Jo Riddett was born in Cheshire and now lives in Hampshire. She has written three previous novels, *Children on the Shore* (1986), *All a Green Willow* (1990) and, available from Headline, *On the Way to the Wedding* (1994).

Praise for *On the Way to the Wedding*:

'Wry, understated, remarkable for its sure sense of period, how people thought and felt in the 1920s; it makes for a love story with an agreeably ironic zest' Nina Bawden

'It is truly English – with what Jo Riddett calls the "English light", different from any other ... There seems to be a touch of E. M. Forster here, particularly *The Longest Journey*' Penelope Fitzgerald

After the Fair

Jo Riddett

First published in 1995
by Hamish Hamilton Ltd

First published in paperback in 1996
by HEADLINE BOOK PUBLISHING

10 9 8 7 6 5 4 3 2 1

ISBN 0 7472 4978 4

Printed and bound in Great Britain by
Cox & Wyman Ltd, Reading, Berks

HEADLINE BOOK PUBLISHING
A division of Hodder Headline PLC
338 Euston Road
London NW1 3BH

For Alexandra Pringle

A day after the fair: old country saying meaning 'too late'.

It is never too late to learn what it is always necessary to know.

1678 Sir Roger L'Estrange
Seneca's *Morals*, III, xx

Wednesday

THE FAIR WAS COMING BACK to Peapod Field. Beyond the hedge the five-acre site was being prepared; voices carried questions and advice; a measuring tape was realigned; a tractor delivered its trailer-load of baled straw; a lorry inched through the gateway, another waited in the lane, engine thrumming. Much ado in this backwater, more than for many a year. Thirty, to be precise. Thirty years since the last Peapod Fair. Gledwyn watched a moment longer. Adjusting his grip on the walking-stick and remembering to limp, he set off back to the house.

He left the lane and hobbled on to the gravel drive. Two hundred and twenty laurel-lined yards, this winding drive. So, every time he travelled it both ways he had covered quarter of a mile. Quite enough to demand of a man of his years and condition. Round the first bend he paused and lit himself a cheroot.

If asked, Gledwyn would have explained that a while back in the winter he had broken his ankle and it still bothered him. Old bones. At seventy plus you could not expect to bounce back like a three-year-old. True, the X-ray showed a neat, successful restoration, all the more remarkable for there having been a previous injury to that joint: 'You've done very well, Mr Geddes! Been very lucky all things considered! We'll have you in full working

3

order in no time. Nurse will show you the way to the Therapy Unit.'

All very well for them to rejoice. X-rays don't show pain. Nobody could tell how much pain he had to bear. Some days, he told himself, were less trying than others; which was as far as he was prepared to go in modifying his claim to pain. And the invalid status had brought with it one undeniable benefit: the presence in residence of his sister, Connie. She had come to tide over, between housekeepers. Mrs Bale, so aptly named, had quit, praise be. Bossy old bag. Little sister Connie was a decided improvement. Not a bad sort, Connie.

A pick-up truck rumbled towards him and he shuffled aside, against the laurels. Presumably the delivery that Con had mentioned. Fair-day paraphernalia. Trestles or something.

The driver geared down, steering by. 'Cheers mate!' he called, voice raised above the racket from the radio in the cab.

Gledwyn watched it go, the din hanging in its wake. In his rare ventures beyond the bounds of home he had encountered this feature of late twentieth-century travel, the stereo blast and blare, frenetic assault, charging the highways. According to Con, it was common now in shops and pubs as well. She reckons that people nowadays are afraid of silence. She once said that thinking has become a minority sport. The sort of thing that Con comes out with sometimes. Not a lot to say for herself usually. Quiet type. Odd cove. Quiet, though.

He took a final pull on his cheroot and rubbed it out beneath his foot on the gravel. The last curve of driveway brought him limping on to the broad sweep before the house.

It was not a pretty building. Impressive in its way, no doubt, with the charmless grandeur of Victorian railway architecture, northern variety, imposed upon this gentle downland border of south Wiltshire over a century ago. Grandfather Geddes had been one of those self-made Victorians, a Bible and Brass man from the gritty breeding grounds of Merseyside, who had made his packet selling tinned meat to various armies. This house was his brain-child and testimony to his labours.

'Wickenwood,' he had been wont to say, 'is built from honest hard work and good British meat!' – an utter-ance that had filled the infant Gledwyn with confused alarm. It had been a release from horrid dismay to ascertain at last that those were not dehydrated flesh but ordinary building bricks. A century of wind and weather had gone some way towards subduing the overall hec-tic flush, and white paint in place of bottle-green had leavened the woodwork in later years, but even the strivings of Virginia creeper had failed quite to soften the visual impact.

Inside had fared better. In Betty's day. Betty's blithe and wholesale refit, once Gledwyn had inherited; third generation, his father interred beside grandfather in Dymp-ton churchyard down the road. Betty's day.

Gledwyn halted, dug the packet from his cardigan pocket and lit himself another cheroot, drawing deep. His face took on the lines of surprise and injury appropriate to recollection of the wife who had gone away, eighteen years ago. He moved on. His mind veered from that past and to the immediate future. With a small intense surge of pleasure he made his way towards the privacy of his study, and the bottle awaiting him there.

Connie ran her eye over the stacked trestle tables in the coach-house. Pity. But there it was. The hire firm could not deliver them direct to the site on Saturday. Too busy.

'Busy time of year, lady! Functions all over the shop – August y'see. Half a dozen same day as your lot – twinning binge at Chelstock, county flower do, ballooning, jousting, veteran car rally – you name it, not to mention a couple of weddings! Let's hope there's someone left to come to your do, eh? Sign this would you? Cheers!'

Not 'mine' actually. Actually, Collingford Antiquarian Society's. Some of whose members would presumably now have to come into the yard on Saturday. Oh, well. So what? She'd be bound to meet some of them in the Peapod, anyway. She and Gledwyn ought to put in an appearance. Along with the rest of the family.

She liked the smell of the coach-house. She always had. Leather, grain, paraffin and apples. None of those things remained, but by some magic, the smell lingered on. Beyond the trestles the shafts of the old pony trap canted above its brittle shell: the redeeming feature of those obligatory holidays with Grandfather. The jiggling rides to Dympton village, the gardener's boy plying the reins,

6

whistling between his teeth, and then the barley-sugar twist to suck on the way back, donation from Mr Gosse the grocer for Little Miss Geddes.

Against the further wall, under dust-sheets, the old Armstrong Siddeley saloon, still up on blocks from 1942, petrol rationing, when Father had to take to bus and train. Black body-work, walnut dash, and green leather upholstery. No one had ever got round to disposing of it; Father had bought a Wolseley after the war.

From iron pegs set in the brickwork, in a shroud of cobwebs, hung the frame of the sit-up-and-beg upon which she had learned to bicycle – adjudged 'healthy exercise' and therefore permitted. Though not, *not* on Sundays. On ordinary days. Wobbling round the yard and down the drive between the laurels, but not beyond the gate. Whose had it been? Not Grandmother's for certain. Mother's? In her youth? A question that had not at the time occurred to her. She just used it, whenever possible, a blessed escape from the cold but stifling house, the grown-ups, and Gledwyn's covert tauntings, sibling tiffs. Later, after they had come to live here, she had ridden it to school sometimes in summer, if she was staying late for choir, or tennis, or going to tea with a friend in Collingford, staying too late for the last bus round the villages.

They had come to live here when Grandfather died, because then Wickenwood was Father's. She liked the outbuildings all right, and the bicycle and the hill called the Mullen at the back, but the gloomy house dismayed her. They had to come, though. Something to do with a tail. Later to clarify as 'entail'. About which Father was highly gratified. You could not say pleased, since Father did not go in for pleasure. There was a funeral at Dympton church and then Father being 'highly gratified', her first adult phrase, she supposed. He stood upright, back to the fireplace, thumbs in his waistcoat pockets, addressing his silent wife and two children, the thirteen-year-old Gledwyn in particular, upon the honours and responsibilities of stewardship, which turned out to mean living in this house and now being head of the family business.

Heads and tails. Promoted from the Bristol office, to be Head, at Wickenwood, from where he commuted in the Armstrong Siddeley to 'HQ', the buildings beside the railway halt a dozen miles away. Wearing a homburg hat. He had a different one, paler grey, for church on Sundays. Same sour expression. Different hat. She had missed Clifton. They had lived in a high house backing on to the Downs in a leafy avenue of other high houses, near the park and the shops and the schools, and people. Mother had become even quieter at Wickenwood. Silence, without tranquillity, was what Connie remembered of childhood at Wickenwood.

With her left hand she scooped up the two mugs in which she had brought tea to the trestle men, and with her right hauled the high doors shut. In the yard was Gledwyn. Back from his constitutional, doing his limp.

Gledwyn was seven years her senior, but that somehow did not confer seniority. Even in childhood she had seen him as simply older. Size, weight and gender lent him

8

advantage in nursery tiffs, that was all. Later, in middle life, when promotion arrived it seemed only to diminish him. As head of the house and head of the firm once Father had died, Gledwyn seemed to dwindle, overwhelmed perhaps by the monstrous task of supplanting Arnold Geddes. Connie could see with hindsight how much Betty had supplied in tact and discretion from behind the scenes. When at last she left him, he seemed totally surprised; and more indignant than shattered: 'I don't know what she's thinking about!' Petulant. But then Gledwyn, as one who had never in his life asked questions, much less sought answers, would not be likely to understand what anyone might be thinking, least of all his wife. Connie could remember their wartime wedding. Uniform suited Gledwyn, in every sense. He looked dashing and handsome; and Service life took care of everything, good, bad and indifferent. Connie guessed that those years had been the best for Gledwyn – downhill all the way since then. Civvy Street. He met the decline by lowering his expectations. And abandoning any attempts at gratitude. For some years now the height of a day's achievement lay in communion with his whisky bottle. The business and its responsibilities had long ago been passed to Roy, the son he found 'priggy', and who lived with his wife and family in London. From time to time and without giving attention, Gledwyn appended a signature to papers Roy dutifully sent. And that was about it, really. Gledwyn's life. Connie reckoned she knew more about Gledwyn than he knew about himself, or than did anyone else, except Betty. Betty would not perhaps go as far as Connie in saying that, after all, Gledwyn might not be able to help being the flop he was. But then Betty did not have Arnold for a father. Connie had often thought that if there was something less desirable than being Arnold Geddes's daughter, it must be being his son.

She had been here now for seven months, having come to hold the fort for a few days back in February. Mildly irritated, partially resigned, she watched her brother doing his martyred hobble across the yard. All part of his cunning and absurdly transparent scheme to keep her there. Affection played little or no part in his motivation. What mattered was that he found it easier having Connie at the helm than any hired housekeeper. He didn't have to 'cope' with Connie. With employees, one had to cope: 'not the same thing at all!' he had said, expressing approval for her presence, the closest he had come to managing gratitude. He had just turned down an applicant. There had been three responses to the advert Connie had devised in the spring, and he had turned them all away, found shortcomings. 'Wouldn't do – wrong sort altogether!' Connie had reminded him that she did have a house to go to. She missed her modest and peaceful home sixty miles away. He had fidgeted, ducked and mumbled about it making better financial sense for her here at Wickenwood. 'All-found, expenses paid . . .' She had told him, half cross, half amused: 'If I wanted a career as a housekeeper, Gledwyn, I'd apply for one through the usual channels!' But she knew that secretly he relied on seduction by drift: the passage of time to wear down her resistance, a touch of moral blackmail with the 'poorly foot' to help things on their way. Exasperated, but not quite immune, she said to herself, 'Tiresome old humbug.'

She set off across the yard with the two empty mugs and the delivery chit in her hand. Two dozen trestle tables, for some aspect of Saturday's Fair. The produce tent? There would presumably be a produce tent? She knew little of the details; only that this Peapod Fair would approximate more closely to a village fête than to the old Peapod Fair. She reflected that the circumstances which had brought her here in February had – by drift or by necessity – detained her too long. She could do without this coming weekend. Gledwyn had done the right thing when he agreed to the reinstatement of the Fair – it could and should have been reinstated years ago, an innocent and convivial local event – but she would have preferred to leave the Peapod Fair where she had last encountered it, well tucked away in the past.

She'd see the family, of course – offspring and their offspring – and that rated a welcome of a sort, though Gledwyn would not agree. 'Dread Octopus': his view of the family. Gledwyn liked it best when nothing whatever occurred to disturb the dust on a low-profile lifestyle. Truth to tell, at the moment, so did she.

She came alongside Gledwyn. 'Getting on with it in the Peapod, are they?'

'Measuring-up and so on. Pardey's man's there with a load of bales. Yes, taking shape, taking shape.' He began a laborious ascent of the kitchen step.

'Trestles've arrived,' she said.

'Uh-huh. Saw the lorry.'

'Coffee?' she said, following him in.

'Hmm? Er – no thanks. No thanks, Con.' He limped across the kitchen. 'Think I'll just go and have a little rest. Little rest before lunch.' He was gone, into the study.

Connie went upstairs to resume bed-making with Mrs Persey. Mrs Persey was a blessing. A woman of almost no words, she turned up in her gleaming Morris Minor two mornings a week, discharged her duties with exemplary competence and departed at twelve to her home somewhere the other side of Dympton. She had appeared in answer to Connie's card in the Post Office window back in March. She was therefore unacquainted with the visitors arriving this weekend. The last family gathering had been the usual three days at Christmas, and the rooms had not been used since then. Connie had made out a list with names for ease of reference. Three bedrooms were now complete – the one for Roy and his wife, Eithne, the one for their two large adolescent sons, Alistair and Adrian; and the adjacent little room for their youngest, Cecily. Mrs Persey was seeing to the blue room; Connie's daughter Rowan and her husband were to be in here.

Mrs Persey said: 'I've done the attic room except for the bedside rug, and that's on the clothes-line.'

'Oh, OK.' The attic was by tradition Ruby's room: Connie's granddaughter now in her mid-teens, one of Rowan's two children. The other, Teddy, was on school camp and would not be coming. Of the rest of the clan, Connie's son Malcolm and his lot would join Saturday lunch but would not be staying overnight. 'That's it, then, isn't it? Good. Soap and towels in the bathrooms? Thanks, Mrs Persey.' She would be here again on Friday morning for a last whip round before the troops began to arrive.

Downstairs again, Connie unpinned a list from the cork board. Gledwyn's contribution to hostmanship, the order for Farraday's Wine Merchants, Collingford. By the entry for claret he had written 'Decent, not plonk', and 'Ditto ditto' by the order for six bottles of white. Usual whisky. Gin and ton.

Connie had told him that people seemed to be drinking lager these days.

'Do they?' he had said. 'Good God!' and told her to do whatever she thought fit in that line.

She jotted down 'Lagers'. She would ask Farraday's to recommend a brand; she knew nothing about lager. She wrote 'Cokes + Robinson's squash' and wondered how many of which she ought to ask for. Roy's lot would not be having Cokes – Coke contained E things and was taboo. So that left Ruby, and Malcolm's two. Well, then. A couple of six-packs will be plenty. She phoned the order through.

From above came the diminuendo wail of the vacuum cleaner. Almost twelve o'clock and time to put Mrs Persey's money out. But first . . .?

Not on any list but very present to her mind, another call she ought to make. She looked at the phone. Get it done with. She lifted the receiver and dialled a Collingford number. Over the years it had acquired three extra numerals and a code in place of COL.

She delivered the information that the trestles had arrived.

Duty done.

She went to sort out Mrs Persey's money.

IN A GREEN AND PLEASANT corner of old Collingford the Antiquarian Society concluded the meeting designed to put the finishing touches to Saturday's arrangements. The dozen or so people did not see themselves as a committee. They were old friends, known to each other for donkey's years, even in some cases since schooldays before the war. Such meetings as were necessary from time to time were held in one or other comfortable home. Today's was in the sitting-room of Alec and Elinor Hennessey. Elinor had just taken the phone call from Wickenwood.

'All's well!' she passed on the information. 'That was Connie Bruce – the trestles have arrived OK!'

Gerry Kepstow who had recently bought a four-wheel-drive Daihatsu Fourtrak – 'handy little job!' – was looking forward to putting it through its paces on Saturday, ferrying the trestles to the Peapod and thereafter plying the refreshment tent with casks of water drawn from the stand-pipe in Wickenwood's driveway. He had plenty of offers of help for the lifting and shifting.

Everyone present had known Gledwyn and Connie since way-back-when, though none of them had been in touch with either for years, not until a few months ago when Gledwyn had been approached by letter for permission to reinstate the old Peapod Fair on Geddes land: '. . . a bit of community fun, a touch of education about the communal past, and a few quids raised for the Scanner Appeal . . .' Permission had been granted, all right, but with it came no invitation to renew acquaintance and drop in at Wickenwood. No. The Wickenwood drawbridge, so to speak, had been raised against intruders after old Mrs Geddes's death a couple of decades ago, and remained raised, even though Connie was back there now.

In the course of the preparatory meetings this past summer, the friends had restored lost memories of Connie Bruce, née Geddes, pieced her history together: how she had been widowed back in the late sixties, sudden and shocking death of Oliver from a heart attack after a squash game, and he only early forties; Connie devastated, naturally; and left with two kids in their teens. How she had coped wonderfully, stayed on in Twickenham until the children were through school and university, then moved to the Cotswolds — was it the Cotswolds? There was a general impression that it *was* the Cotswolds — gutsy thing to do, making a fresh start for herself. Never remarried, obviously. Well, they were devoted, the Bruces. And — let's face it — Oliver Bruce would be a hard act to follow. Such a personality, such a star turn! And now here she was back at Wickenwood looking after Gledwyn.

Gledwyn had broken his ankle in a fall last winter and then broken it again — such rough luck! And bones don't mend so easily in the over-seventies, eh? The official account maintained that he had slipped on black ice outside the kitchen door, but private opinion had reservations . . . old rumours returned to mind, of Gledwyn taking to the bottle when his wife buzzed off. Anyway, black ice or booze, the housekeeper out there at Wickenwood quit, and who could blame her? Too much responsibility altogether. Obviously in recent years Gledwyn had become a bit of a liability. Rather tough on Connie having to pick up the tab, eh?

Elinor would have none of that: 'Oh, *goodness*, no! It's company for her as well!'

But then, Elinor was rather inclined to dismiss any hint of what might be deemed less than positive. She was an ardent disciple of the creed of Positive Thinking. There had been, just after the war, a flurry of books and articles emanating from the broader reaches of Popular Philosophy in the United States, commending the Power of Positive Thinking. Elinor was not so much a convert as a 'natural' – a duck, as it were, already in the limpid and lovely buoyant waters. Though to some the doctrine seemed inadequate to life's realities, it had to be conceded that Elinor presented a persuasive sample of its virtues. At any rate, she was trim, youthful, vigorous. Well, they both were, she and Alec – dozens of grandchildren, but still as nifty as a pair of thirty-somethings, out there on the tennis courts.

Now, turning to the french window open to the grey midday, she cried: 'Oh good! Look – I do believe it's going to rain!' And it was true that perhaps the gardens were a little on the dry side.

Someone said, 'Well, let's hope it doesn't decide to on Saturday, anyway!'

But Elinor pointed out that even if it did there were going to be lots of interesting things under canvas at the

Fair. And on this heartening note, the group dispersed, hurrying off to various lunches before the rain arrived.

The Hennesseys unhurriedly made their way through the understated perfection of the graceful old house and into the wide, flagstoned kitchen. 'Jimmy's perfect for the tannoy!' Elinor said. 'Such a dear – and such a pleasant voice!'

'Good chap!' Alec agreed. He set placemats and napkins at the refectory table while his wife applied vinaigrette to their salad, this being Nariza's day off.

The quiche today was asparagus. 'Delicious!' said Alec.

This afternoon they were off to the garden centre outside Warminster. The new season's bulbs were just in and Elinor was particularly eager to make her purchase of five hundred narcissi, which she and Alec would plant across the far boundary of the lawn – so beautiful in the spring, and such a wonderful scent. 'I'll take those dianthus cuttings along too, darling – we can drop them off at Beryl's on the way back. She's got some hydrangea cuttings for me, you know? Those glorious creamy macrophyllas she has on their terrace. I thought I'd try them against our cotinus – plenty of moisture and shade there!'

Alec agreed that was the best spot. He said he would drop the strimmer off at the repair shop too while they were out and about. Elinor told him about the new servicing unit recently opened on the industrial estate; Jane had told her about it, and it would be a good idea to give it a try, take the strimmer there, wouldn't it. Alec agreed that it would.

'Hope little Roddy likes his prezzi!' he mused. It was a grandson's fifth birthday, occurring this year in Italy, on a family holiday. 'Shame we can't see him!'

'Oh, but we're talking to him on the phone this evening!' said Elinor. 'He loves telephone calls!'

'Bless him,' said Alec, and cleared away the quiche dishes.

The fruit bowl between them, Elinor, peeling a peach, said, 'I've been thinking, darling – we must get Gledwyn and Connie over for an evening. I'll do a supper party. Get them over!'

Alec was scrutinizing his pear: 'Bruise on this one . . .' He applied his knife.

'What d'you think? Supper party, right?' She popped a piece of peach into her mouth and watched her husband for his answer.

'Fine, darling!' He nodded, glancing across at her; but he was engrossed in attending to his pear.

Thursday

CONNIE STOOD ON THE CROWN of the Mullen. It was almost dry beneath the two old yew trees behind her, but the residue of last night's downpour lay in pools across the low land, the fields round Dympton, Lottismore and Belstock Hythe. From up here she could see the workers in the Peapod, a team hauling on ropes and canvas raising a third marquee, two men spreading straw across churned mud. Shifting her gaze, she saw that she had left her bedroom window open. Well. No harm. The rain had finished, the clouds were lifting to the north; south over Dorset sunlight sifted through. So. Perhaps it would be settled for the weekend. That would be welcome. Better for the Fair of course, but also for temperaments corralled at Wickenwood; family gathering; the weekend's influx.

She ducked inside the skirts of the yews and mounted her childhood roost, the low branch wide as a berth, and propped her back against the ancient bole, her knees drawn up and lightly clasped, the practised habit of a lifetime. Now the roofs and gables of the house were still visible but the upper windows had dropped from sight. As a child in her secret refuge it had satisfied her that though she could see Wickenwood, Wickenwood could not see her. There was a triumph in that. In later life – teens? twenties? – sitting there reflecting on that satisfaction, she had wondered at it, pondered its significance, and came to think that it had derived from a sense of power. Power lay with her. Not with them. The power and the control. Illusory, of course. Delusion. They knew where she was. And always, and usually soon, the summons would split the stillness, the blast on that whistle, commanding her return. It was, appropriately enough, a whistle once used to dispatch men from the trenches, 'over the top' into the fray. Father had kept it from the war. He did not use it for the dogs. Just for his children. She had found that ironically amusing even as a youngster, though the concept of 'irony' came later.

A residual breeze eddied through the yews carrying a snatch of sound, preparations at the site. In childhood she had scurried through the laurels for a quick secret glimpse of these preliminaries. In their way they were as exciting as the Fair itself, and had the added attraction of being ruled out of bounds by Father. It was vulgar to gape, a sign of ill-breeding to be inquisitive. But then, he had hated the Fair anyway, and endured its annual presence only because Grandfather John had always collaborated with the tradition and because no cause to dispatch it suggested itself – until, of course, 1963.

Whoever had written the text to the Antiquarian Society's booklet had a delicate touch. Connie had read it last night. Someone had sent a complimentary copy to Gledwyn. It was handsome, well designed, nice-quality paper, attractive line drawings, illustrations to four pages of text, no name claiming authorship. The information was familiar to Connie, and to Gledwyn, picked up in their childhoods, the history of the Peapod Fair.

The five-acre site has been known as The Peapod time out of mind, the name Peapod deriving from the word Piepowder, which is a corruption of the French *pied-poudreux*, meaning 'dusty-footed', or 'vagabond'. A Piepowder Court was a court of justice formerly held at fairs, which dealt with disputes between buyers and sellers; literally, then, a wayfarer's court.

The reader was told that the site had once been common land, but had passed into private ownership under rather dubious circumstances at the time of the Enclosure Acts of the eighteenth century. The Fair survived though. It had been of prime importance in the district since medieval days, prospering on the wool trade, and it survived the Agrarian revolution, flourishing into the early nineteenth century, even holding its own after the railway came to make Collingford the new centre of local commerce. With the exception of the two World Wars this century, the Fair, notwithstanding fluctuating fortunes, had never been suspended; and throughout, under the aegis of Manor Courts, Courts Leet, or later, Magistrates, JPs, the Piepowder system had continued, arbitrating in disputes, though by the 1930s the presence of the JP at his bench had become a quaint archaism, a symbol of the past without serious purpose.

Connie knew all of this well. She had passed it on to her children, to Malcolm and Rowan, most particularly to Rowan who at Junior School had 'done a project' for History that year, that final year: 'At my grandfather's home near Dympton in Wiltshire he has got a field called The Peapod.' A proud, proprietorial introduction to eight painstaking pages of history well supported by careful drawings, crayoned with the treasured set of Caran D'Ache. She was awarded a prize, quite rightly. It had not sustained her much through the mortification she felt when a month later it was her grandfather who decreed an end to Peapod Fair.

Connie had read the concluding paragraph of the Society's booklet with interest and a smile that was wry. Very tactfully expressed:

The last Peapod Fair was held in 1963, the year in which the death of the field's owner, Mr Arnold Geddes, necessitated reviews of the family estate, one consequence of which was the suspension of the use of Geddes property for purposes of public assembly. Happily, constraints no longer apply, and we are indebted to the present owner, Mr Gledwyn Geddes, for his willing co-operation in the restoration of this intriguing and delightful aspect of our local heritage.

Very tactful indeed! A skilful fudging of the facts, a deft reassembly of the chronology. He *had* died that year. But that was two weeks after he had shut down the Fair in an orgy of righteous indignation. His parting contribution to the sum of human happiness. Perhaps he had died of an excess of moral rectitude. Certainly not of an excess of anything more alluring. Father's regimen of thrift and self-denial admitted of no indulgences – Plain Wholesome Food, Sensible Clothes, Physical Exercise, Hard Work, and weekly doses of castor oil for his children, bowels and their movements having been a special locus of Father's attention. No drop of alcohol, no crumb of tobacco tainted the purity of life at Wickenwood. The annual importation of a beer tent to the Peapod, its cheerful bibbers smiling through the fag smoke over their pints, had long been anathema to Arnold Geddes, the justification of his complaint against the imposition, the presence, of the Fair. And how perfectly had the Lord delivered unto Arnold the Philistines when, in 1963, he learned with unbridled satisfaction that 'Hippies' were smoking cannabis and popping LSD within his precincts. With what alacrity had he telephoned the police. And terminated the Fair. Eight in the evening it was, when the Panda cars appeared. She remembered that, though she had not been there, not at that moment in the Peapod.

Preferring to forget, she fished in her anorak pocket for the hand-out leaflet delivered this morning with the local rag. An invitation to the Fair. A humbler proposition, cheap and cheerful, art-work minimal and rough-and-ready, a sketch of balloons across the top bearing each a letter to spell PEAPOD FAIR plus two exclamation marks; across the bottom a rudimentary map showing the location, and 'Proceeds to the Scanner Appeal'. Attractions duly listed. In the marquees the serious stuff of amateur competition: home-made jams and marmalades, cakes and breads, cordials and wines, and garden produce aspiring to perfection, flowers and vegetables and fruit. A Craft display, pottery and paintings, weaving and embroidery, knitting, lace-making and soft toys. For the punters' participation, the enduring favourites: Lucky Dip, Hoopla, Raffles and Donkey Rides. And more recent additions to alfresco high-jinks: Welly Throwing, Bobsleigh, Bouncy Castle and Laser Clay Shoot. Bowling? Yes. But not for a pig. No doubt Animal Rights and cholesterol consciousness had between them altered perspectives. Thirty years. A long time. Plenty enough for perspectives to shift ... She shoved the leaflet in her pocket and ducked away from her tree and the snare of recollection.

She stood a moment flexing stiffness from her back, and set off down the Mullen. The marquee was in place, the tractor chugging across the Peapod, a couple of cars – one arriving, one departing – in the lane, much busyness. She stepped with care down the steep wet path. Haul that stuff out of the freezer to begin its slow thaw. Ten for lunch and supper tomorrow. Fourteen, Saturday. Like Christmas, as Gledwyn gloomily observed. His Dread Octopus. Well it was certainly true that families produced freaky and unpredictable dimensions from time to time. A lot of unruly emotions lurking, in family circles.

She let herself through the wicket gate and stooped between the overhanging shrubs. In the yard before her a car stood with its doors open, a suitcase on the gravel.

'Rowan!'

'Oh, hello, Mum!' Her daughter, emerging from the kitchen.

They met mid-yard. In the brief embrace Connie had time to note that Rowan was as thin as she looked, as she was told: 'I know you didn't expect us till tomorrow but something's come up. I thought you wouldn't mind. Knowing you, everything'd be ready weeks in advance anyway. OK?'

Rowan was already striding away, picking up the suitcase: 'I'll be back tomorrow, naturally.'

'What is it?' Connie followed in her wake. 'What's happened? What's wrong?'

'Wrong?' Rowan led into the kitchen. 'Nothing's wrong! Sheila rang me,' she said. 'I'm going to Sheila's for the night – her birthday party – the Big Four-O. You know?'

Sheila was a friend from Rowan's university days and witness to Rowan's register office marriage as Rowan had been to hers; Sheila now lived in Yeovil.

'Just worked out right – being down here these few days – practically on the doorstep!' Rowan put down the suitcase, faced her mother. Coolly, she said, 'Well, it's all right, isn't it? You don't *mind*, do you?'

'No – er – no! Of course not! Er . . .' Connie glanced towards the door into the hall, 'Is Clive –?'

'He's not coming.' Rowan hitched the suitcase, moving on.

'Not coming?'

'He's tied up this weekend. Couldn't make it. Teddy – well, you know that already, he's on school camp in Wales – just Ruby and me this weekend.'

Ruby materialized in the hall doorway.

'Hello, Ruby!' Connie greeted her.

'Hello.'

Ruby, like her mother, was dressed in jeans, T-shirt and sweater, but, unlike her mother, cut a dishevelled figure: podgy, unkempt, even slightly grubby, Reeboks unlaced, hair uncombed, face beneath it flaccid and pasty.

Rowan dumped the suitcase at her feet: 'Here – you can take it up.'

Over her shoulder she asked, 'Usual room?'

'Yes – er – yes! Ruby's attic!' Connie found herself

29

attempting joviality. Ruby gracelessly lugged the suitcase away, clumping towards the stairs.

'Actually, Mum,' Rowan produced a smile, 'I wonder if you could keep her here a day or two after the weekend, she'd love a few days down here, they get so bored at home! Anyway, we can sort that out tomorrow. Must dash!'

'What? Now?'

'I'm late already – rather a last-minute rush . . .'

'You'll at least have a cup of something, surely? What time does this party start? It's only three o'clock . . .'

'I know, but I'm giving Sheila a hand – food and stuff for tonight!'

'Oh,' said Connie. 'Well,' she said, 'what time tomorrow, then? You'll be here for lunch.'

'Oh, doubt it! Sleeping off the after-effects, helping to clear up.' And she was off into the yard, slamming car doors, fishing keys from her pocket. 'Make Ruby pull her weight!' she called. From behind the wheel she leaned to direct a smile: 'And . . . thanks, Mum!'

The tyres sprayed gravel, accelerating away.

Friday

GLEDWYN SHUT HIMSELF IN HIS STUDY, relinquished his stick and slumped into the armchair.

Roy's voice, instructional, carried from the hall. Trundlings and twitterings diminished, suggesting that the walkers, duly organized, had been marched off for their dose of good clean air. Gledwyn gloomily mused. His son, with every passing year, more closely resembled the late and unlamented Arnold. By some masterstroke of genetic quirkery, Roy had been denied any variant characteristics, had hopped a generation and emerged as distressingly pompous and priggy as his paternal grandsire. Not much hope for the fruit of Roy's loins either by the look of it – trio of conformist priglets. But then Roy had taken unto himself a wife who even now, at the age of forty-two, wore white ankle socks. Not much hope for the offspring.

As rarely as possible Gledwyn recalled his own wife and the far-off yesteryears of family life, but this weekend memories heaved and twitched in their shrouds, summoned to resurrection by the clamour in the Peapod. In spite of himself he thought of Betty now, wondering how she fared with Roy and his lot on the rare occasions when they met. Not Betty's cup of tea at all. But since she lived in West Virginia, USA, it presumably was not much of a problem. Stella, now – she was a different case altogether. The emigration of their daughter to marry her sheep-farmer in New Zealand had been a blow to both her parents. Pick of the litter, Stella. Typical of life that of the two it should be Roy who remained within these shores . . . But then, he was going to inherit Wickenwood, of course. Entail. First the founder, Grandfather John, then Arnold, now Gledwyn himself, soon Roy, and then Alistair. Or was it Adrian? Gledwyn never could remember which was which, equally featureless youths. Was that Alistair, the one next to him at lunch who had tutted at Connie for offering Coca-Cola on the menu? Yes. So the other one was Adrian. Being coy and cocky about his 'remarkable' exam results. Cecily presented no problems of identification, being the girl. The one with plaits. Who had brought her recorder because she did not want to miss her daily practice and was only sorry that there was no piano at Wickenwood because she would have to miss her daily practice on the piano and in a month's time was to be taking her Grade Six! Grade Six, mark you. Pause for applause. Connie had obliged. Cecily had wanted to know if Ruby was still learning the flute. Ruby had answered 'No.' The only word she had uttered throughout the meal.

Down in the dumps, young Ruby. Gledwyn pondered. Con says Rowan wants Ruby to stay on next week and that Ruby wants to stay. Doesn't look to me like someone who wants to stay. Looks pretty fed up to me. And what about Rowan? Rowan looked rum yesterday. High as a kite. Rum.

The reflective process threatened to disclose problems. He shut his eyes, lay back, and slept.

He roused to the sounds of television. Someone watching television in the sitting-room next door. Who on earth? He peered at his watch. Quarter past three. Who? Not Roy and his lot that's for sure, too much like self-indulgence, telly-watching. And anyway they're out there somewhere. Breathing fresh air. Who – oh! Ruby. Must be Ruby. Must have skived off from the health-giving walk very sensibly. He lit a cheroot. As kids go, Ruby's OK. Nice kid. Going through a monumentally unattractive phase just now, looks like an unmade bed, but she's OK. More sense than to ruin a remarkably fine lunch by flogging off across the countryside. Jolly good lunch it was; unfortunate company and in the wrong room, but a first-rater.

Lunch had been taken in the dining-room at the conference-sized table. Gledwyn much preferred the usual arrangement – tiffin for two, in the kitchen, something on Radio 4. He had never liked the dining-room, associated as it was with formal family gatherings throughout his life. Didn't like the room. Aesthetically it had improved under Betty's administration. He conceded that. Betty had gone through the house like a cleansing fire once Father had popped his clogs. They had lived for what seemed eternity in a welter of brick dust and trailing wires, paint cans and plaster and ladders and artisans swarming in overalls. Betty throve. Mother wore an inscrutable expression. Neither child seemed put out, only Gledwyn identifying with the cat and the dogs who drooped in unfamiliar corners waiting for the nightmare to pass. When it did, it was undeniable that the result was a triumph: 'You can actually see in here without the lights on all day!' came the cries. 'There's actually something to sit on that doesn't dislocate your vertebrae!' some outspoken visitor had felt free to observe. It had, of course, cost a bomb. Betty had dismissed 'penny-pinching'. 'We're not going to spoil the ship for a ha'p'orth of tar,' she had declared, bent above the Sanderson samples. Several thousand pounds' worth of tar was nearer the mark. But it was true that the transformation was miraculous: colour, light, warmth, where once arctic twilight had prevailed.

Not that she'd stayed long to enjoy it.

Extraordinary thing. After thirty-one years. Just like that. Off she'd gone. No explanation that he could understand. Always seemed all right to him. Women. No knowing. Can't have been all that bad, the old connubial state, because she took a second plunge later.

Never felt the need himself. No. Well. Hadn't made all that difference, Betty going. Things ticked along much the same really. OK these last few years, retired, pottering along. Jolly nice. OK. Specially since Con moved in. Handy in the cookery department, and a great improvement on those warder types with their pinnies and their eyes sliding about monitoring the level in the whisky supply . . . Cold ash fell from the cold cheroot and softly collapsed across the carpet. He slid back into sleep.

'Gran said to bring this.'

Gledwyn blinked awake and straightened his spectacles, focusing on Ruby who stood heavily in the doorway holding a cup and saucer. 'Oh . . . Gracious! Must have nodded off – tea, is it? What's the time? Come in come in – thank you – yes, put it there, would you?'

Doing so, she slopped tea into the saucer. 'Uh. Sorry,' she mumbled.

'No worry, no worry!' Gledwyn fished a tissue from his cuff. 'Hold the cup a mo'! There we are!' He mopped the saucer. Ruby handed him the cup. He took a sip, said, 'Watching telly?'

'No. Yeh – well, I was. They're all in there now.'

'Oh, back from the walk, are they?'

'Yeh.'

'You having some tea, then?'

She didn't seem to be going; neither could it be said that she seemed to be staying. She was just – without momentum; in transit but impaired, like a vehicle afflicted with a slow puncture.

'I don't want any.' She collected herself and trailed towards the door.

Watching her leaden progress, Gledwyn found himself saying, 'Why don't you get yourself a Coca-Cola and drink it in here with me?'

Something within the proposal kindled interest – its practical agenda, filling tedium of space and time, or, perhaps, its conspiratorial tang – and she cocked her head: 'Yeh! OK!' she said and almost smiling almost hurried into action.

She must in fact have attained a remarkable turn of speed, for she was back in a trice, bearing two cans of Coke and swiftly shutting the door upon the hootings of a recorder warming up.

'That's the ticket, that's the ticket!' Gledwyn waved her to a chair. 'Take a pew – oh, and there's a tumbler on the sideboard.'

Ruby fizzed open a can. 'Don't need one,' she demonstrated, expertly swigging. She drank deep.

'Thirsty!' Gledwyn chuckled.

She nodded. 'Well,' she said, 'I don't like squash and the water here tastes funny.'

'Does it, does it? Never noticed, myself. Dear old South Wilts Water Board.'

'I 'spect it's recycled,' Ruby told him. 'It's better than home, but I 'spect it's recycled here too. London water's recycled millions of times – recycled from sewage.'

'Good God!'

''Tis, honestly. We did about it at school.'

'Disgusting!' Gledwyn pondered the information. 'Must be all right, I suppose, can't be poisoning folk and so on. Disgusting, though.' He thought about it. 'Don't suppose they do that here, y'know. Have to in London, not enough water, too many people – horrible place, London.'

'Oh no, London's great,' Ruby assured him. 'Just the water's awful. London's great.'

'Not been there for years.' Gledwyn pursed his lips. 'Must be ten years or more. Like a madhouse then. Couldn't get across the street for traffic, folk pushing and shoving, nothing where it used to be. Used to be all right, London, years ago. Jolly good before the war and so on.' He smiled at his great-niece: 'Place for the young, eh? I'm past it now.'

Ruby smiled back at him. 'Yeh – well, *I* like it!' Then she added vehemently: 'Plenty going on there,' and scowled.

Gledwyn caught the gist, said kindly, 'Unlike here, eh?'

Ruby flushed: 'Oh – I didn't – er – it's very nice here! I mean, I just meant my friends are all in London!'

'Of course, of course!' Gledwyn reassured her. 'Understand, quite understand!'

'Well there's this gig tomorrow, y'see,' said Ruby in further explanation.

'This – ?'

'Gig! You know? *Gig* – music – a group!'

'Ah! *Top of the Pops* sort of thing?' Gledwyn had glimpsed this televisual event while flicking through the channels.

'Right!'

'Well . . .' he offered dubiously, 'something of the sort at the Fair tomorrow – a band, of a sort . . .'

'Oh – the *Fair*,' Ruby's disdain was entirely dismissive.

'No good, eh?'

'I wanted to go to that gig – really wanted to go' – she was scowling again – 'but Mum wouldn't let me stay. I could've stayed with Cassie, but she wouldn't let me!'

'Friend, Cassie?'

'Yeh.'

'Well' – Gledwyn felt he must be diplomatic – 'your mother must have her reasons!'

'Oh *yeh*!' Ruby sneered. 'She's got about a million reasons – she's "got things to do", she "won't be home", and Dad's away and she's not leaving me in the house on my own and she doesn't like "Cassie's influence" all of a sudden. She's never been snotty about Cassie before! And anyway, I've got to go to this bl –' She checked, modified: 'I've got to go to this Fair,' she grumbled to conclusion.

The bowed, aggrieved head touched a sympathetic

chord in one so frequently aggrieved. He discarded diplomacy: 'Rotten luck!' he said. 'Rotten luck, old thing. Families, eh?' He sighed. 'Tricky things, families . . .'

She looked up, curious, surprised, interested.

'Oh yes . . .' Gledwyn wagged his head: 'You know what they say, you can choose your friends, but families – those are just dished out! Luck of the draw, parents, children . . .'

There was a small silence, awkward in a way, but also alive with reciprocity.

'Yeh!' said Ruby, and smiled, an endorsement.

'Hmm!' Gledwyn sealed it with a smile of his own. He glanced at his neglected cup, sat himself forward. 'Tell you what,' he confided, 'my tea's cold, and anyway I could just do with something more lively, eh?' He made to haul himself upright but Ruby said, 'I'll get it! What d'you want?' and was on her feet.

'Well, that's jolly decent! Yes! Well – how about a touch of the old usquebaugh? Over there.'

At the sideboard Ruby hesitated: 'Oosker . . .?'

'Usquebaugh! Whisky!' he explained. 'Proper name for it, Gaelic word. Yes, that's the chappie! That's it – a dash more . . . Whoa! That's it. And a touch of soda – merest touch. Whoa! Splendid! Gaelic, y'know, usquebaugh – "water of life"!'

Handing it to him, Ruby said, 'It smells all right, but it tastes awful. I like vodka – oh, I don't want any now, I'm just saying, I like vodka. Rum's good too, rum and Coke.'

'Oh no no no!' Gledwyn deplored. 'Horrible stuff, rum!'

'No, t'isn't,' she laughed. 'It's great!'

'Well, I haven't got any, don't keep it.'

'No, I don't want any now.' She fizzed open her second can of Coke. 'Cheers!'

'Cheers!'

Gledwyn took a pull at his drink. 'Er – how old are you now . . .?'

'Fifteen,' she said gloomily.

'Don't like being fifteen?'

'Well, you can't do anything.'

Gledwyn slid her a sly smile: 'Seem to manage, though? Vodka? Rum?'

'Oh *that* – everyone does that. I mean really do things, without being nagged all the time.' Wandering in vague inspection of the room's contents, she stopped before a framed photograph, black and white, a line of posed persons, hanging on the wall. 'Who're these?'

'Mm? Oh. Family.'

She peered: 'That's *you*!' she cried. 'You're in the army!'

'The RAF.'

'Jeez! Were you a pilot?'

'Rear-gunner – in the back of a bomber – chap in the tail.'

'Wow . . .!' Reverentially she said, 'That's dire – I saw it in a film. All bunched up and *freezing*!'

'It was!' cried Gledwyn, gratified. 'It ruddy well was – fancy you knowing that!'

'It was in this film on telly – the rear-gunner got shot and the others tried to get him out, only he was jammed in and the wind was terrific and he was covered in blood! Really gross! Ever so sad,' she giggled nervously, 'because they got him out but he died anyway. It was really sad. He had this dog – you know, back at home, only he didn't come back and the dog kept waiting. It was on telly, the film.'

'We crash-landed once,' Gledwyn offered in lieu of having heroically died.

'*Did* you?'

'Made it back on one engine – flak, y'know, over Cologne. Had to crash-land. Ruddy miracle, really. First-rate pilot. Jolly close call.'

'I'm glad you got back!' Ruby flashed him a warm smile and peered again at his portrait. 'Golly! weren't you thin!' she said. 'Who's that? Is that *Gran*? It's *Gran*!' she marvelled. '*Is* it?'

'Bring it over!' Warmed by whisky, Gledwyn waved an expansive arm: 'Take it down and bring it over! Years since I looked at the ghastly tribe!' He adjusted his spectacles, propped the frame on his knees: 'Yes, that's Con, that's right!' Pageboy hair-style, flowered cotton frock, sandals, a 'cheese' smile on her face.

'How old was she?' Ruby hauled a leather stool along-side and settled.

'Ooo . . . 'bout sixteen, seventeen. End of the war or thereabouts – summer of '45. Still at school, of course.'

Ruby scanned the company. 'What gruesome clothes . . . Except the uniforms, they're all right . . .' There were several of those. Gran appeared to be the youngest present. 'Everyone's standing at attention!'

'Oh – that's the daunting influence of Father.'

'That him?'

'That's him. Ghastly head of the ghastly tribe!'

Ruby giggled uncertainly: 'He looks –'

'Like a ghoul!' said Gledwyn with relish. 'Jolly good likeness too! Mmm,' he mused, 'Mother made excuses for him occasionally – said he'd had "a bad time in the war", First World War, y'know. Well, maybe he did and maybe he didn't, but he certainly enjoyed his bit of authority. Hung on to his uniform – First Lieutenant – wore it round the house. Oh yes! *And* made us go out "on parade" – oh, it's true! Stood us in the yard, Con and me, doing deep breathing exercises. Thump between the shoulderblades for "slacking"! Oh yes – nasty temper.' He pointed to a dumpy figure in the photograph: 'Best description of Father I ever heard was from her – Aunt Audrey, his sister, y'know. Said he was a disciplinarian without any self-discipline. Yes. Nasty combination, that. Oh – and he had "direct contact with God"! Yes. Very handy. Always right, y'see.' Gledwyn chuckled, took a swig of whisky. 'Kept a cane to whack us with. Kept it in here, the study. Court martial! Whack whack, quoting the Bible! "For the good of your immortal soul", y'see.'

'That's *dire*! You mean – Gran? He whacked her, too?'

'Oh yes! Oh yes! Mind – Mother put a stop to that. I'd gone in the Forces by then. Con was thirteen. Mother told him it wasn't right, not for a girl of thirteen. Wasn't right for a boy come to that, but anyway, Mother stopped it.'

'Why,' said Ruby indignantly, 'didn't she stop it before?'

'Mm? Ooh . . .' Gledwyn shook his head, frowned. 'Frightened of him, I 'spect. Under his thumb. No self-confidence, nervous type, Mother. Got round to it eventually. When I'd gone.' He took a gulp of whisky. 'She meant well, meant well . . .' he muttered without conviction, and set the subject aside.

'Now *that*,' he said jovially, 'was Uncle Gerald. The Knitter! Yes – mad about knitting! Very good too – made Fair Isle pullovers, dozens of 'em. Fair Isle – you know? Fancy patterns? Yes. And he was married to that one – Ethel. Odd cove, Ethel, talked to herself a lot. Well, p'raps it was all that knitting, click click click, eh? And that's Dan – their son – my cousin, in the RAF same as me. He wasn't a bad sort, Dan. Bit of a stuffed shirt. That's his wife, Maureen – well, fiancée – they married when he got demobbed. Both dead and gone now – older than me, lot older than Con . . .'

Released and inspired by replenishments of usquebaugh and Ruby's enjoyment, Gledwyn expounded, talked on. There was Aunt Mavis, who always wore a hat, indoors and out and doubtless also in bed – that very hat; maroon felt thing it was. There was Uncle Vincent who wouldn't walk under a ladder and met his Maker being run down by a van, having stepped into the road in observation of his superstition – well, so the story said, might even be true! Cousin Ralph: 'Now, he went missing on Snowdon in a fog; out all night; great hullaballoo – search parties, police – very high drama! Till he was found bunked up nice and cosy in a cave with a girl he'd taken a fancy to at the Youth Hostel! And that's Blodwyn. Yes, Blodwyn! Well, there's the Welsh connection – my mother, she was the daughter of a farmer in north Wales: that's why I've got this Welsh name, yes! Blodwyn trained for ballet, but grew and grew, six-footer, so that was that. Joined the Land Army. Later on married some old widower chappie and off they went to Canada or somewhere. Aunt Nora. She was an army nurse in Palestine in the First World War – married a Greek, liked her fags. Disapproved of by the family ... It was the gardener who took the photograph, trembling in his boots lest he got it wrong! Anyway, he didn't – he got it right – hand didn't tremble at any rate! Dead and gone now like most of us. One or two still alive – me, Con, Megan – that one there. And that one – forget her name – well, she was alive last Christmas, and Megan. That's how you know when you get to our age – when the Christmas cards stop coming you know they've popped their clogs. Jolly good system, Christmas cards, serve the purpose!' He was all smiles.

There were some he had missed. There was one, a pretty blonde one in uniform: 'Who's that one?' asked Ruby.

'Mm? Oh.' The smile slid off his face. 'That's Betty.'

Ruby clearly ought to know. But didn't. 'Erm –?'

'My wife. As was.'

The mists cleared. 'Oh!' said Ruby in a hushed tone. She felt the need to excuse her clumsiness: 'I never met her, she must've died before I was born.'

There was a small silence. 'Died?' said Gledwyn. '*Died*?' And then suddenly he was raging: 'She's not dead – not she! Buggered off! Very much alive if you please!' He was shouting. 'Buggered off and left me! Left me! Left me! *Dead*? Not she! Not bloody well dead! She's bloody well alive, she is! *Alive*!' Sweat stood on his brow.

Ruby blenched. 'Oh – oh – oh!' she whispered. 'Oh God!'

Gledwyn was not hearing her, being too surprised by the force of his own emotions, hearing only himself, the outrage, the expletives . . .

'Oh – oh! I'm so sorry – oh, I'm sorry – I didn't know! Well, I got muddled – I – oh! I don't listen – everyone tells me I don't listen!'

But Gledwyn was staring bemused through an alcoholic haze at the images of fifty years ago, the youth, the certainty. 'Damnedest thing . . .' he murmured. ''straordinary. Just took off. No warning. Suitcases, coat on in the hall. "I'm off!" Didn' know what she meant, didn' know what she was talking about – 'd never said anything – always seemed all right to me! Just like that . . . Just – took off . . . Never said a word before.'

Ruby was in extremis, dismayed by her *faux pas*, moved by the evidence of pain. 'Oh God,' she murmured. 'Please – I'm sorry – I didn't know . . .' Involuntarily she touched him, patted his arm. 'Uncle?'

'Mm?' He seemed to come to. He blinked. 'Oh, no no . . ,' and he was patting her, comforting the comforter. 'No no. Not your fault, eh? Families!' He sighed. 'Not the sort of thing they'd talk about, eh? Skeleton in the cupboard and all that.' He sighed again. 'Old hat, anyway. Don't suppose anyone ever gives it a thought, 'cept me.'

They sat in silence, hands clasped. Ruby said, 'No. I didn't know. No one's ever said. I'd have remembered that . . .' She said, 'Cassie's mum's divorced. She left him.'

Gledwyn nodded sadly. 'Lots of that these days. Divorce.'

'I know.'

'Mm.'

'They came to us first. After the bust-up, Cassie's mum and Cassie and Nita. They stayed with us. Till they got a place. They've got a place now.' She said, 'Lisa – Cassie's mum – she was Mum's best friend.'

'Help a friend out, eh?'

'It's cooled off now.' She said, 'Lisa's nice.' With sudden energy she said, 'My mum's crackers!'

'Oh – er . . .' Gledwyn demurred, 'friends, y'know – fall out sometimes – tiff, that sort of thing . . .' He gently detached his hand, set the photograph aside, propped it by his chair.

Ruby ventured to ask: 'Are you – er – y'know – divorced?'

'Mm? Oh yes,' he said resignedly, passion expended. 'She wanted a divorce. Married another chappie.' He said, 'Later, you know. Lot later. Didn't leave me for the other fellow. Met him later . . . Don't know why she left me . . .'

'She's gone to this party.'

'Mm?'

'Mum.'

'Yes – er, yes. So I understand.'

'She's always going off now.'

'Erm –'

'She's always going off on her own.'

Gledwyn shifted, swirled the drink in his glass: 'Well, erm, I suppose your dad's busy – pretty busy, eh?'

'No,' said Ruby simply.

Silence followed. It seemed to demand conclusions, but neither, apparently, was prepared to proceed beyond that unequivocal 'no'. Perhaps instinct drew them back from a path that could lead away from the companionship and solace of the past hour.

And then the door flew open. 'Oh *there* you are!' Rowan's irritation was etched in her angular stance. 'I've been looking for you ever since I got back! What are you *doing*? *Everyone's* out looking for you!'

'Well I was *here*!' Ruby flashed back.

'She was here with me!' Gledwyn helplessly sounded guilty. He attempted defiance: 'That's all right isn't it, eh? Little chat with her great-uncle?'

Rowan shifted her stance, came up with a quick smile: 'Tst! Sorry, uncle! Of course – only *really*! Everyone's looking everywhere! Poor old Alistair trudged up the Mullen!' She made a small deprecatory laugh. 'Well come on, then! They're all waiting!'

'What for?' Ruby didn't move.

'We're playing Monopoly before supper. Hurry up!'

'Oh *God*!' cried Ruby.

'On your feet – quick about it!'

'*I* don't want to play Monopoly.'

'No arguments. Come on!'

Ruby slouched to her feet. She traipsed to the door. At it, in passing, she caustically inquired, 'Nice party?'

Rowan flicked her head aside, 'Very, thanks!' she replied.

Saturday and Other Times

I

Eithne collected a large bowl of potato salad and bustled off again.

'That one can go on the sideboard!' Connie called to her.

'Righty-ho!' sang Eithne.

'This one, Mum?' Malcolm indicated the platter resplendent with salmon mayonnaise awaiting dispatch from the kitchen.

Connie glanced at the clock: 'Actually, Mac, you could be rounding people up for me. Would you?' She swooped on the olive oil and dripped some more into the vinaigrette. 'Lord knows where they've all disappeared to . . .'

'Some of them went off down to the Peapod.' He made for the door. 'I'll take the car.'

Down to the Peapod! Fine time to be going off to the Peapod! Connie applied the whisk. Sod's law? Murphy's law? Somebody's blooming law: folk draped all over the kitchen all morning so you can't move, and as soon as the meal's ready to eat – they all vanish! She set the vinaigrette aside, wiped her hands on her apron and carried the salmon through to the dining-room.

'Oh, it *does* look lovely, Auntie!' Eithne always called her Auntie. Connie had from the outset invited her nephew's wife to call her Connie, but for some reason that degree of familiarity was never achieved. Perhaps some deeper wisdom prevailed: Eithne remained true to her personality, quaintly childlike, and the relationship between the two women had not been thrust into closer intimacy than it could realistically, in the long run, bear. They got on well together, Auntie and Eithne, meeting on the common ground of practicalities, kitchens and kids, humdrum, necessary domesticalia. Connie had learned to value Eithne's reliable energies. Suddenly and almost venomously, so that fractionally it seemed that she had spoken aloud, her mind declared: Pity I can't say the same for my daughter! Where the devil has *she* been all morning!

'. . . made a jug of lemon and barley,' Eithne was saying. 'I thought that would be best – save getting up and down to the sideboard!' She said, 'Anything wrong, Auntie? Have we forgotten something?'

'Oh – er – no! No . . . Just – checking. No – everything's here! Just the salads to dress and bring in. That's splendid, Eithne. Thanks! I'll just go and see to the salads, then . . .'

She had woken early. She had not felt rested. The slight headache was still lurking. Perhaps she would take some paracetamol. She preferred not to on the whole, but this was – what? two days, now. Getting tensed up. Quite unnecessarily. Everything under control on the domestic front. Emotional front? Well, she had thought all that through, and whereas she was not exactly looking forward to meeting all the old crowd again – specially not the Hennessey pair – it was only a matter of an hour or so, a few social platitudes and it would all be over, such as it was. The past could go back into the past where it belonged. So. Nothing to have a headache about! And yet. And yet, unease persisted. Of course, there was the

Ruby factor. She was concerned about Ruby, who looked a real mess in every way; seemed – well – unhappy . . . But then was this not classic adolescent dementia? Reeboks, dreadlocks and Sony Walkmans – but essentially the same affliction of all generations. Her own, fifty years ago; Rowan's, in her time . . .?

A twinge pinched her forehead. Maybe she would take a pain-killer. Or perhaps she'd be all right after her morning tea.

She had been revived by the tea; and the morning had gone well. Mission accomplished, and lunch on the table as requested by quarter to one. Slightly irritating to be hanging about now, but not catastrophic, the menu being what it was, nothing to spoil in the waiting. She rooted about and found the spare tin-opener. Might as well see to that now. Malcolm and family were en route to a self-catering cottage in the Quantock Hills. Philippa had said she'd forgotten the tin-opener. She could take this one. Mac had told her, 'There'll be one there!' but Philippa said they should buy one today because you could not be sure. They had bickered about it. Both a bit tired, in need of the holiday. She gave the tin-opener a thorough scrubbing under the hot tap. The kids seemed all right, anyway. Isobel and David. Both grown another couple of inches since Christmas. Isobel's adolescent dementia seemed less acute than Ruby's. And her appearance was a deal less defiant; her protests were registered in blue nail-varnish and double piercing for rings in her ears, which her parents had forbidden but she had accomplished all the same. In other respects she was really quite elegant, and at sixteen set fair to become a very comely young woman.

David of course was still, at thirteen, a child, still absorbed by such innocent diversions as skate-boarding and cycling. His bike and Isobel's were strapped to the roof-rack. Isobel had expressed her disdain: 'Can't see the point, taking bikes to the Quantocks, never get out of bottom gear, anyway. Well I shan't use mine. Dad can use it. All boys together.' She had further made her opinion of family holidays plain, not abashed to lower her voice as she informed Ruby that she was 'really pissed off' and that this was 'but positively the last time' she was going to be dragged along. Connie dried the tin-opener and gave it a buffing with a clean tea-towel. Good as new. She put it on the sill where she would see it and remember to give it to Philippa. They wanted to be away by four-thirty to get settled in at the cottage, so they would spend just a couple of hours at the Fair, then have a cup of tea and push off. They'd stay at Wickenwood overnight in two weeks' time on the way back; more leisurely, and with luck, more relaxed. Mac looking quite washed out, overtired. And greying, a touch of grey, at the temples. Forty-two. My God. Forty-two . . . Time's wingèd chariot. Doesn't seem forty-two years . . . That seedy nursing-home, reluctant recruit to the emergent Welfare State. The stroppy night-sister. Cassidy. Sister Cassidy who had found her in the corridor at two o'clock in the morning and sent her back to the ward: 'Contractions? Rubbish! You're not having contractions! Get back to bed, Mrs Bruce!' And thirty-five minutes later, Malcolm. And Motherhood. And the curious closed world of babies: breasts and burps and nappies and nerve-ends. And certainly no notion of Motherhood extending to a man with greying hair framing a tired face. Motherhood was a condition identified with prams and playpens, and later, school reports and parents' evenings and performances of *Noyes Fludde* and the standard funny bits from *Midsummer Night's Dream*, and at Christmas time the carol service. Later still, it ran to careers and all those pamphlets – university, college, tech, which? and why? Along the way, some fun, some tedium. Fits and frights from time to time. Hostilities; but also pleasures, satisfactions, and sometimes fellowship. But never, as far as she could remember, was Motherhood a condition once entered never left. She supposed she had supposed that when they 'grew up' – well – that was it, really. At any rate, she had not considered that Motherhood would one day extend to a man of middling years. 'Or to a bold, assured woman, striding across the yard ... Way back among the bootees and the bibs, that had not been part of her understanding ... And what of Fatherhood? What had been Oliver's understanding?

She found that she was there beside the sink, and holding two tea-towels. And was back to the present, carrying with her the hovering eminence of Oliver. Familiar and elusive. In death as in life, there but never there. Absentee landlord. And still she could not extricate herself from all that. Even now, still sad and angry.

It took effort to pull back from the sadness and the anger. It always did. She made the effort. She moved herself, hung up the tea-towels, rearranged her face, hearing footsteps in the hall.

'All right then, Auntie?' Eithne appeared, pink and busy. 'Everything's ready I think. Oh, and I've borrowed the chair from the hall – good job nobody's superstitious! Thirteen at table! Gracious!' She looked about. 'Where is everybody?'

Connie smiled: 'Oh, they've disappeared off somewhere. Mac's gone to round them up.'

'Tst!' said Eithne. 'Aren't they naughty! But I find that, don't you? Just when it's all ready – they all vanish into thin air!'

'I was just thinking that myself,' said Connie. 'Yes!'

'Sod's law!' said Eithne surprisingly and giggled, a deeper shade of pink.

Delighted, Connie laughed. 'That's the one!' Eithne – white ankle socks, latched sandals, dirndl skirt and white blouse – looked all of twelve years old, and wholesome as a sweet nut.

'Oh, here they come!' she cried. Mac's car trundled into the yard bringing Adrian, Cecily and David.

'Daddy's walking up with Alistair,' Cecily announced in the kitchen. 'Well – they're jogging up! I've been stroking the donkeys, Mummy! They're so sweet! But I'd better give my hands a really good wash!' And off she trotted to the cloakroom.

Mac, shepherding Adrian and David, came in: 'Roy's on his way, with Alistair.'

'But where's Rowan?' Connie flushed. She had almost shouted. She gave a swift unconvincing laugh. 'And the girls,' she added, producing a rueful smile. 'I mean we did say twelve-forty-five sharp!'

There was more than a touch of irritation in Mac's reply: 'Rowan and Philippa have gone off somewhere. Don't ask me, ask Roy. He told me.' He prodded the boys ahead. 'Go and get your hands washed, Dave – and put a comb through your hair.' To his mother, he added, 'And the girls are hitching back on the truck.'

'Truck?'

'Land-Rover thing. Well it's been up and down and round the yard all morning, shifting those trestles. Alec Hennessey and another old bloke. Move *on*, Dave!' He chivvied off into the hall.

'Ooh,' said Eithne, 'Mr Hennessey! How nice! I've not seen any of the Hennesseys for ever so long!' She stood on tiptoe peering through the window into the yard. 'They're such kind people, aren't they?'

Connie managed to find voice: 'Yes.' She faintly flushed, shifty with insincerity.

'Oh, there it is – ooh, what a smart truck!' and Eithne hopped off into the yard.

From within the kitchen doorway Connie watched her flag down the driver and saw Isobel and Ruby emerging from the back of a sort of pup Land-Rover.

She retreated a step, but not before the man at the wheel had seen her and raised a hand in greeting. She raised her hand.

The girls ran in: 'Sorry, Gran!' They flurried to the sink: 'Can I move this, Gran?' A colander of lettuce.

'Yes.'

'We've been helping!' Isobel ran the tap, and both girls, very giggly, sploshed and jostled, washing their hands.

'We're going to help with the water this afternoon!'

'Hauling bales . . .'

'*And* heaving trestles! Phew!'

Some *sotto voce* remark from Isobel and peals of

laughter, a snort, a couple of words: 'Quite fanciable . . .'
And more mirth, sploshing and splashing and foam from
too much washing-up liquid.

Eithne came skipping back. 'Well!' she said. 'He's just
like he always was. Hardly any older – all these years!'
To the girls she said, 'He says you were a real help this
morning! Isn't that nice!'

This drew further giggles and snorts but Eithne seemed
not to be aware and went on: 'Did you see your mums
anywhere?'

'No!' they shrugged.

Connie brushed past Eithne. ''scuse me.' She crossed
the hall and let herself into the study.

'Ah – lunch?' Gledwyn stirred, glass in hand.

Connie closed the door behind her. She went to the
sideboard. 'Well, lunch *is* ready,' she said, 'but not everyone is back.' She clunked a tumbler, poured an inch of gin
and swashed tonic on it. She took a gulp. 'Ugh. No ice.'

'AWOLs, eh?' said Gledwyn warily. Unlike Con to lay
into the gin at this hour.

'Mm?'

'AWOLs – absent-without-leave-ers. Late for lunch.'

'Oh. Yes.'

'Tst – nuisance, eh?'

'Oh it's up to them,' said Connie. She sat herself on the
desk edge. 'Done my bit.' She drank more gin.

'Ought to keep some ice in here,' said Gledwyn. 'Used
to do that, didn't we? Sort of thermos thing . . .?'

'Mm? Oh. Yes.' She was flicking through the local rag
beside her on the desk. 'Would've liked to've gone to
that,' she said.

'To . . .?'

'The County Flower Show. It's today.' She shoved the paper aside.

'Mm. Shame,' Gledwyn murmured neutrally. What's upset her, then? Something's given her the pip. Quite glum. 'Flowers and things at the Peapod, aren't there?' he offered. 'Flower tent?'

'Uh-huh.' Unimpressed. She drained off the gin. 'Tastes vile without ice. Tepid gin.' She dumped the glass on the desk.

Gledwyn took a quick look at his sister's profile. Down-in-the-mouth; and the gin's not hit the right spot. 'Yes . . . yes . . . If you're going to drink gin, you need ice! We'll get that thermos thing back into use, eh?'

There came a tap tap at the door and Eithne's head appeared saying apologetically, 'They're back, Auntie!' and nodding encouragement.

Gledwyn watched his sister rearrange her face into a smile and depart, saying, 'Oh, thanks, Eithne! No harm done. Nothing to spoil, was there?' Determinedly jolly.

He softly grunted, collecting his stick and draining his glass. Always the same, complications, aggravations, with these family gaggles.

'We're very lucky,' Eithne was telling Philippa across the table. 'Our greengrocer sells organic vegetables. Well, he wasn't keen because they *are* more expensive, but we persuaded him, our Women's Group. He teases us! "The Yogis," he calls us because we all do yoga together! And he's coming round to organic apples and those citrus fruit without those nasty chemicals in the skin – well, you use

grated lemon peel in all sorts of things, don't you?'
Eithne lived in Wandsworth. Philippa lived in Finchley.
'Have you got a good greengrocer?' Eithne wondered.

Philippa assured her that they had and added that
anyway most supermarkets had an organic section these
days. Alistair was instructing his grandfather on the disci-
plines of Computer Studies, undeterred by minimal response. Isobel, between mouthfuls, was imparting some
information *sub rosa* to Ruby, who was giggling. Connie
glanced at her granddaughters. They seem to be hitting it
off. Ruby's cheered up, praise be . . .

Connie was monitoring the progress of the meal, now
into the main course. The roulade went down well;
salmon disappearing, so that must be all right. Cherry
and almond flan ready in the fridge. Likewise tonight's
casserole. Spuds for baking ready and scrubbed, so nothing more in the preparation line to do today. Connie had
eaten but little herself. The ache was returning to her
head.

'. . . wrong vehicle for the job!' Roy was announcing.

'Four-wheel-drive,' Mac suggested without much interest. 'For getting about rough ground.'

'The Peapod is hardly rough ground!' Roy told him. 'I'm
surprised the organizers didn't think it through. One pick-
up truck could have moved the entire load in one delivery.
As it is, the Daihatsu Fourtrak made twenty-four separate
journeys, one trestle table per trip, and in the process
churned up a great deal of mud – not unnaturally, given the
ground conditions following Wednesday night's storm.'

'Well, it's drying out fast. Hot day,' said Mac, politely
closing the subject.

But Roy had not finished. 'The damage unfortunately is done. And matters are not likely to be improved, since I gather that water is to be transported to the site this afternoon using the same vehicle. Add to that the impact of two thousand visitors, and you have a recipe for a quagmire! I was quite surprised that Mr Hennessey had not thought of that. But he doubtless meant well.'

'Yes, I was saying to Auntie they are kind people, aren't they?' said Eithne. 'I had a word with him. Such a long time since we saw him, but he doesn't change, does he?'

'And how long do you judge that to be, eh?' Roy assumed an air of sagacity. Roy was proud of his memory. Demonstrating its superior force was a favourite exercise. So when Eithne ingenuously replied, 'Ooh, well, it must be six years ago, dear, because Nicola was expecting little Roderick!' Roy was not best pleased. Denied his coup, he cleared his throat, said, 'Correct!' rather irritably and went on, 'He does seem to be in remarkable health for a man of his years, and considering the detrimental regimen imposed by the demands of his career in business that is all the more remarkable – irregular hours, unregulated diet.' He frowned in concentration: 'What is the expression? Ah! "Jetting". Jetting about the world – all these factors impose strains on the system.'

'That's particularly damaging,' Adrian explained to the company and began to expound the measures taken by airlines to safeguard the health of aircrew crossing time-zones.

Philippa collected up empty nearby plates and slid away murmuring to Rowan, 'Let's clear, huh?' and

Rowan joined her. Adrian was on to blood-vessels and cardiovascular disorders; Ruby was stifling mirth, Isobel smirking.

Connie pushed back her chair: 'More salad anyone?' she interjected.

Adrian paused only to assure her that he for one had had an elegant sufficiency before resuming his dissertation. Connie gathered up a pile of dishes and sidled away.

The wide hall was cool, washed with the gentle apricotty light reflecting from Betty's pretty painted walls. From the kitchen ahead Connie heard, 'Blimey! What a pompous pillock!' Philippa's voice, and snorts of suppressed laughter. Then Rowan's voice, low and rapid, Philippa's responding: 'Mm ... mm ... Yes! No of course not! ... Mm ...'

Connie momentarily slowed. She clanked the dishes she carried, and, having thus prepared them for her entry, made it. An aura very like that surrounding Isobel and Ruby, part salacious, part subversive, entirely clandestine, hung a moment and snuffed out as Philippa rounded a smile on her and said, 'That was fabulous, Connie! Another winner!' and Rowan busied herself at the sink.

'There's pud yet,' said Connie pleasantly. She left her crocks on the table and went to the fridge. 'Oh, by the way, there's a tin-opener over there on the sill. It's a spare, so you can have that.'

'Oh!' said Philippa. 'Well, actually – that's very kind, Connie, but I bought one in Collingford this morning.'

'Well, that's all right, then,' said Connie equably and lifted forth the cherry and almond flan.

Rather boisterously Philippa cried, 'Wow! Look at that! Heaven help my waistline!'

Connie smiled obligingly as she took herself and the flan out of the kitchen. 'Bring the cream, would you?'

'. . . I think you will find it was 1958,' Roy was saying.

'Mm, probably,' said Mac.

'1958. Auntie can confirm that? We were just recalling Stella's accident,' he summoned his aunt's attention, 'the injury to her head at the swimming-bath. April 1958, unless I'm very much mistaken.' A circumstance beyond imagining, to judge from his serene expression.

Connie sliced the flan, calculating portions. 'Oh, I expect you're right . . .' She lifted a wedge and slid it on to a plate. Eithne passed it down the table.

'It was a Tuesday,' said Roy. 'It was a Tuesday, because it was market day in Collingford and market day is on Tuesdays. And I am certain of the fact that it was a Tuesday because Mr Hennessey had difficulty in conveying Stella to the hospital. He had to take the longer route as the marketplace was closed off for the day. Mr Hennessey drove your car, Auntie, and you accompanied Stella. She was bleeding profusely and showing signs of having suffered concussion. I, being the eldest, was left in charge in your absence. I made sure that everyone dried and dressed themselves – it was a chilly day. Christopher and Rachel Hennessey were of the party – indeed that is how it was that Mr Hennessey was present, he had brought them along; they had of course walked, their home being no distance from the swimming-bath. And so it was that it must be your car which was used to carry

Stella to the hospital. Christopher would be nine years old, Rachel five. You, Malcolm, were seven, and Rowan – ah! there you are, Rowan! We were just recalling Stella's accident at the swimming-bath and seeing who among us could place the date.'

'When she smashed her head? Don't ask me!' Rowan plumped herself down. 'All I can remember is gouts of blood.' She passed her flan across to Isobel. 'This is too much for me.'

'Ah,' said Roy, 'I had not supposed you would be able to *remember* the date – you were merely four at the time – but rather whether you could *place* the date!' He raised a hand against the proffered cream-jug. 'Not for me, thank you.' He went on: 'Now, Father! Surely you can place the date?'

Gledwyn blinked from the depths of bottomless boredom and replied, 'No.'

'Oh, come! Come, come!' Roy waxed jocular. 'The year of my tenth birthday? I was ten that year! I had reached double figures and you and Mother had given me my first wrist-watch and advised against my wearing it to the swimming-bath, though I persuaded you that I was confident that it would be quite safe, as indeed it was. Auntie, here, kept it for me in her handbag during the swimming. And that,' he told them all, 'is how the incident can be exactly placed in time. My birthday falls on March 30th. The visit to the swimming-bath was the first that year, since, being an open-air bath, it had just opened, following Easter. It was the first occasion on which I had worn my wrist-watch to the swimming-bath. Ergo, April 1958. There are,' he told them, 'always means

64

and methods with which to place past events if one is prepared to take the trouble.' He took up his spoon. It seemed possible that he had done with Stella's accident.

In case he hadn't, Philippa, who had rejoined the table, struck out for new ground and loudly addressed her children: 'We'll be off at four-thirty, you two. So be back here by four-fifteen, OK?'

As a measure to silence Roy, it was a failure. Itineraries were high among his favourite themes. 'What route are you proposing to take?' he inquired of Mac.

Mac roused himself. 'Oh. Um, via Taunton.'

'Taunton, eh?' Roy frowned. 'Surely the Bridgwater approach would be the better choice? Considering the season? You would be less likely to encounter heavy traffic on the more northerly route.'

'I don't think there's much in it,' said Mac, and took another spoonful of flan.

'You propose joining the A303 then? At the junction with the A350?'

'That's right.'

Roy pursed his lips. 'I think you will find that to be unwise. We certainly avoided the A303 on our way down. I consulted the AA – I take it that you are a member? I took advice, was glad to have done so. As predicted there was severe congestion on the A303 yesterday according to the radio report. There has only to be one break-down or one accident and a tail-back of several miles accrues in no time. There was one such yesterday on the Mere by-pass section apparently. You' – he turned to Rowan – 'can no doubt testify to that. Your route from Yeovil will have taken you via Sherborne and Wincanton, past Mere.'

Rowan took up her glass and ducked, taking a sip. 'Mm! Oh – no – I – came back another way!' Connie heard it, the falsity in her daughter's voice, the lie invented.

'Ah! the A30, then?'

On her feet, Rowan said, 'Oh I never know the numbers. Coffee? How many for coffee?' She was on her way to the door. 'I'll make for six anyway.' She was gone.

Philippa swept up a couple of plates and followed her: 'Yeah! Coffee for me!'

Connie sat motionless. A throb beat, tripped and beat again in her head. The truth unfurled itself. Rowan. Oh, my God. Rowan ...

'Are you all right, Auntie?' A whisper from Eithne as Roy droned on.

'Oh! Yes. Yes! I'm fine! Fine.'

'... and there bear left, taking the B3153 through to Langport ...'

II

They had gone. Gone to the Fair. Connie had managed it: 'I'll stroll down shortly with Gledwyn – no, really! Do go ahead! I'll have a wash and brush-up and potter along with Gledwyn.'

She lay on her bed, shoes and all, her hand over her eyes. She had taken a couple of paracetamol. From the

Peapod came the tannoy's call to some ticket-holder who had won a raffle.

Behind her hand, within closed eyes, the imprint of Rowan's head ducked over the glass, knuckles tight under thin brown skin.

Thirteen for lunch. Clive not here.

Connie pushed off her shoes, footed them on to the floor and turned on her side. She wanted to sleep. A total oblivion please before the rest of the day.

Sleep would not come. What came were memories, a long, long rolling wave of unleashed memories.

She had known of course. From the moment she had set eyes on her daughter in the yard two days ago she had known. It takes one to recognize one? A woman on the loose . . .

> When lovely woman stoops to folly and
> Paces about her room again alone,
> She smooths her hair with automatic hand
> And puts a record on the gramophone . . .

T.S. Eliot. 1948. First encounters with the intellectual godheads of post-war illuminati. Eliot, of course. Freud, of course. D.H. Lawrence, of course. Pick-and-mix for your sexual mores. Beware repression! Deadly stuff! Only look at your parents' generation – joyless unions clamped in cant! Hail the sexual liberation! Sex is good for you. Good in itself, and good for you. Ah! So . . . another Duty, then? Write out one hundred times: 'I Must Have Sex and I Must Enjoy It.' The route to Happiness, the new Truth. Kick over the traces.

No small print to tell you that you may thereafter spend much of your life trying to find them again, since this route too was a false trail.

Later, much later, she had come across the original of that famous line of Eliot's. Goldsmith had composed it, two hundred years before; she came across it, the elegiac quatrain:

> When lovely woman stoops to folly
> And finds too late that men betray,
> What charm can soothe her melancholy,
> What art can wash her guilt away?

She did not have to commit it to memory. It engraved itself.

They would all be there this afternoon. The past, in force. The Everetts, the Kents, the Jamiesons, the Kepstows. The Hennesseys. Alec. And Elinor.

It was Oliver, with his scabrous wit, who had awarded Elinor 'the intellect of a retarded prawn'. August 1958. 'Imagines she holds the wisdom of the universe, having picked up some half-baked platitudes from a *Reader's Digest!* Positive Thinking!' He was laughing, high on disparagement, fluent on Hennesseys' wine, driving back to Wickenwood. 'She wouldn't recognize a Thought if she fell over one!' He had broken into song, the car swerving and squealing through the midnight lanes: 'Looking on the bri-i-i-ght side of life!' he sang. 'Oh yes! All you need is a large vat of syrup and Death where is thy sting? Never despair! Elinor has the recipe: take a hundredweight of stupidity, a serene and vacuous smile and a large vat of golden syrup. Avert eyes and pour. *Voilà!* Life is *lovely*! Nasties? What nasties? I wonder what she's done with Auschwitz and Buchenwald? Need a lot of Positive Thinking there, Elinor!'

Connie had laughed too. Flown with Hennessey wine and ever susceptible to the extravagances of Oliver's invective mode, she had laughed. The onslaught had little or no weight with Oliver. He was just rather drunk, a word-artist enjoying his creations, not interested in the Hennesseys. 'He's OK as bourgeois Englishmen go, but she's a twit . . .' Connie had laughed, immoderately, with reservations humming in her brain. Oliver had been his party best, liberally entertaining, harvesting the Hennesseys' applause and admiration, flattering and flattered, successfully impressive. The Hennesseys were impressed, oh yes. Thrilled to be hosts to this doyen of the Arts, a name to conjure with in those pre-telly days, a genuine Name and Intellectual, producing, editing and writing for the Third Programme at the BBC, *au fait* with the great and famous. There was to Connie something almost endearing, certainly *ingénu*, in their eager, uncritical acceptance of Oliver's every word, their shocked, excited gasps when Oliver, casually mentioning Larry Olivier, Flora Robson, lightly referred to them as 'mummers'. Four decades ago this was audacity, piquant to provincial ears. Oliver relished his platform, dispensing intimacy, ravishing his audience. They were not to know that this was Oliver's strong suit and greatest weakness, stage-intimacy, capturing each fresh gallery, discarded as the curtain fell. For the Hennesseys that dinner-party yielded a promise of lustrous friendship: 'Oliver. You know, Oliver Bruce? Oh yes, *great* friend, marvellous man!' For Oliver it was over as he drove from their cobbled yard heading back to Wickenwood. 'He's OK as bourgeois Englishmen go, but she's a twit ...' Connie's laughter had been for the rout of Elinor, whom she had found irksome for no particular reason, though Oliver had now provided one, gift-wrapped. Hitherto in their short acquaintance, initiated by their various children splashing into childhood friendship at the swimming-pool that summer – hitherto, Connie had just assumed they had a personality clash or something, she and Elinor, nothing in common, different types, of no consequence anyway. But a dinner-party had been pursued by Elinor once she had discovered that Connie Bruce was the wife of Oliver Bruce and that Oliver Bruce was briefly joining his family's holiday at Wickenwood. That dinner-party had amplified Connie's irritation, raised it to antipathy, and she laughed immoderately – ha-ha-ha-ha-ha! – swaying in the car.

The submerged reservations lasted longer than the laughter.

There were two.

One was familiar, a decade into their marriage: the bleak evidence of deficit, so much on offer, so little delivered, in relationship with Oliver.

The second was not familiar; quite new. She did not truthfully go along with the cheapening of Alec Hennessey. He had been very nice to her. He had asked her about herself, herself, not Oliver. He had lit her cigarettes. Attended to her. That midnight, even as she brayed with laughter, she was not unaware of the flickering potential for treacheries to Alec's wife more mischievous than heartless mirth.

From the Fairground came the thumpa-thumpa of lumpy music, the Air Cadets' Brass Band doing its afternoon stint. She rolled over, sat slumped on the bed. Time to mobilize Gledwyn. Time to make a move. She made none, though.

III

She had met Oliver at a pub in Chelsea. He was ex-army, demobbed and resuming a BA course at London University; she was at a teacher training college in leafy south London. It was 1947. She was there because schooldays were over and she had not known what 'to do'. The clutch of undistinguished School Certificate results and the two mediocre 'Highers' supplied no indication one way or another as to Vocation. She knew she did not want 'to be a nurse', that other staple for spare females. Some Geddes cousin or other lived in Croydon and this appeared to have been the deciding factor, an outpost of authority near by 'to keep an eye on' her while she attended college up the road. So it is that our fates are cast, or so she often afterwards thought.

She came to be in a Chelsea pub as late recruit to a bunch of fellow students going into town that Saturday in search of sophistication. They found it, in a way. The posse of males from the university crowding the bar were ex-servicemen, dead sophisticated if you were hardly yet out of gym-slips. Certainly more interesting than ping-pong in the common room or the student dances laid on in the Assembly Hall and patrolled by college staff.

Chelsea, the West End, Soho! The Odeon Leicester Square; Rita Hayworth all cleavage and legs and sultry eyelids, and in the back row of the balcony some necking. Some more necking, only rather less, in arty little cinemas showing arty and 'intellectually satisfying' foreign films with sub-titles. Afterwards, beer in a pub, and talk – almost all Oliver's, almost all compelling, to artless, unversed ears. He asked her about herself, occasionally, her background, a few questions. He had impressive, trenchant rejoinders, hefty with psychological insights. After the beer and the talk talk talk, back to Victoria and the solo journey, last train out, and the fraught ten minutes' tip-toeing, tapping, whispering and clambering, skulking back into college. Decidedly unsophisticated.

The Easter vac hove into view. Oliver had a couple of times expressed a curiosity, half-a-mind interest, to meet 'your Gothick progenitor'. He now said, 'I'll call in.' He had the loan of an elderly Ford van and was to drive down to Bristol during the vac to collect some furniture from a friend's home, some bits and pieces for the communal basement flat in Earls Court. 'I'll call in,' he told her. She was appalled. Nobody 'called in' at Wickenwood. Nobody. And in particular nobody of the male gender claiming acquaintance with Constance Geddes.

She tried to find words to transmit the vital information

without exposing her childishness and when she couldn't, fell back on: 'I'm not sure I'll be there – I might be out, or away!'

He waved that aside. 'If you are, you are. I'll make it a Sunday and then I can catch a glimpse of the pearl-grey homburg!'

It was all a bit of a joke to Oliver, a passing fancy, amusing. She could only pray it would lose its appeal, be forgotten. Stiff with apprehension she survived the first week and the eternity of the Sunday in which he did not appear. Perhaps, then . . .? She relaxed a little.

Another week. Gledwyn and Betty came for Easter Sunday lunch as per usual. They lived forty minutes' drive away, near Head Office, the other side of Westbury. Connie like her sister-in-law, as a schoolgirl admires a stylish, pretty woman. Betty wore lipstick and high-heeled shoes and clearly did not give a hoot whether Wickenwood approved or not. And at Christmas she gave her kid sister-in-law frivolous presents, accessories to femininity. This Easter Sunday, Betty and Gledwyn had with them their eleven-month-old first-born, Roy, and would not therefore be staying on into the evening. Gledwyn had taken the first armful of nursery paraphernalia out to reload into their car. He reappeared wearing a startled expression: 'There's someone here – a chap – in the yard – for Connie!'

The episode was to take its place in the satirical canon, there to be recalled by Oliver for the delectation of many, not excluding Connie, in the ensuing years, but she had found it wholly unamusing on the day.

Only Betty had the disposition and the nous to dignify

proceedings with some common courtesies. Gwyneth in-
evitably took her cue from Arnold and thereby remained
motionless and mute behind a wild and hapless smile.
Arnold drew himself to the full six-foot-two of military
bearing commensurate with addressing disagreeable and
onerous duties. Gledwyn hid behind the infant Roy,
thrust upon him by Betty who had instantly seen the
social breach and stepped into it, teapot in hand: 'You're
in luck!' she told the visitor. 'Recently brewed and plenty
left!'

'Thank you – yes, I'd like a cup of tea,' Oliver nodded.
Connie, from the door where she yet hovered, pulse
thudding, heard that voice beneath this roof and winced
in submission to the awful fact that he had indeed turned
up.

'Connie?' Betty signalled and summoned her, needing a
clean cup. Connie blundered off to get one. When she
came back, Oliver was seated eating a biscuit and Betty
was developing a conversation. 'Oh, really?' she was
saying. 'Then you'll know the good ship *Ivanhoe*? Trans-
port to heaven, eh? Ah the *relief* of those Saturday
nights!' It seemed that the army had at one point in the
war deposited Oliver in the same dreary transit camp
used earlier by Betty's WAAF unit. The *Ivanhoe* was the
rusty ferry, link with what passed for civilization in
wartime Birkenhead.

Start to finish the visit lasted only twenty-five minutes,
but the sense to Connie was of aeons dense with tensions.
At what point she became aware of the shift, the tilt of
advantage away from the figure frowning on the hearth-
rug and towards the cavalier in corduroys across the

room, she could not later remember, nor work out its source. It was certainly in evidence by the time the Dog Interlude was complete. Bosun, at fourteen, was unsteady on his pins and glazed of eye. Wickenwood had always had dogs, a habit introduced by Grandfather John and followed by Arnold. Arnold did not exactly like dogs, but enjoyed their obedience once trained, and occasionally indulged them with rewards of congratulation, a pat on the head, a word or two on duty and trust, rather in the mode of Victorian sentimental monologue but acceptable to the dog for all that. Bosun had hoisted himself into view and teetered blinking into centre-stage.

Oliver liked dogs. '*Hello!* Who're you, eh?' He clicked encouraging fingers and Bosun swung his traily tail and wobbled to examine whoever it was. Oliver supplied kindly clucky noises and tousled the snuffing head.

'Bosun,' Betty introduced him.

'Bosun!' Oliver grinned. 'And what, may I ask, might you be, eh? Not a mastiff or a greyhound, that's for sure, eh! How about a brach, or lym, or bob-tail tyke or trundle-tail? Hmm?'

Of all present, only Betty and the dog were appreciative of these attentions. Bosun certainly was, and now thoroughly plied his trundle-tail while Betty laughed and wanted to know, 'What was all that?'

Oliver laughed too. 'It's a splendid list, isn't it? It's from *Lear* – *King Lear* – oddly enough. That bit where Edgar's being Poor Tom.' He turned back to Bosun, 'A trundle-tail, that's what you are!'

Betty cheerfully confessed ignorance: 'We didn't do *Lear* at school. Don't know anything about it, but trundle-tail's right enough for Bosun. He's never been able to claim a breed name – have you, old thing? Unvarnished mongrel!'

'None the worse for that!' Oliver assured the dog who was by now capsizing in ecstasy at his feet.

And advantage had passed irretrievably to the intruder. Arnold Geddes was stranded on his own hearth-rug, intimidated by the soupçon of scholarship beyond his grasp and a confidence and humour swelling disconcertingly beyond his control. He remained standing but lost effect. His contribution, when he at last mustered himself, was unimposing by any standards, being merely his routine cross-examination, as with any caller arrived by car, as to the choice and suitability of route.

And then there was the baby beginning to fret and it was time to take him home and Oliver's van must be moved a bit to allow the departure of Gledwyn's car and Oliver said he must be getting along anyway, and it was all suddenly over. And indeed done with. For Arnold made no reference to the visit then or ever. He was no more irritable and blisteringly silent that evening than was usual, but he took his cold-meat supper on a tray in the study. He sometimes preferred to do that. And he did that night. Gwyneth retired early. She was not feeling very well. She did mention the visit. She said to her daughter: 'You ought to have let us know, Connie. That was quite awkward, not knowing.'

Connie replied, 'I didn't know, either!' and flushed, but her mother didn't notice, being on the way out of the room with a cup of Horlicks.

When Betty had left that afternoon, she had taken a

moment to give a nod-and-a-wink to Connie and to
murmur, 'Keep your pecker up, love!' and to add, 'He
seems nice – bright spark!' The commendation, and from
such a source, cheered and emboldened her. The visit
took on a different aspect. Going about the house the rest
of that vacation, she moved with a touch of assurance,
her neck muscles relaxed a little, she felt quite cocky.
They were natural enemies, Father and Oliver. Instant
antipathy. Without a doubt this played its part in warming her regard for Oliver Bruce.

Oliver had enjoyed himself. He enjoyed himself further,
entertaining her with observations culled that afternoon.
It had been, he told her, memorable, and well worth the
diversion from the A303. He heaped excess upon hyper-
bole, delighting her, demolishing for her the fearsome
Gothick progenitor: '. . . the rictal spasm that does duty
for a smile . . . clearly a difficulty for him . . . as though
the effort unseats his liver . . .' And '. . . fatherhood not
really his cup of tea . . . not to be wondered at, given the
demeaning demands of coition. Albeit infrequent . . .' –
Oliver had established that there were seven years between the births of Gledwyn and his little sister – '. . . an
intolerable threat to his dignity, drawers round his ankles
and bum bouncing in the air . . . and no mean trauma for
your poor mother, which explains the evidence of shock
imprinted on her anxious features . . .' Gledwyn was
assessed a sensible fellow since he had acquired Betty,
whom Oliver declared, 'A smasher!' Sharing honours
with Betty, Bosun: 'A dog of distinction!' Oliver told
Connie that she was remarkable inasmuch as she had
survived and escaped the rigours of Wickenwood, though

she was, he explained, father-dominated and too inclined to uncritical acceptance of authority. It was, he told her, a fault she must guard against.

Most of their meetings during the summer were within a group, drinking at riverside pubs, rowing on the Serpentine, fooling about at clock golf, joining and heckling the speakers at Hyde Park Corner, walking the Embankment in the dusk. A couple of Oliver's ex-service friends were going steady with girls – women, for they were six, seven years older than Connie and her peers. When she and Oliver went alone to the cinema he would kiss her, neck a bit, finger her anatomy from time to time in the flickering dark; and, walking her back to Victoria, he would discourse about sex and sexuality and about the importance of truth in relationships, and Connie learned of the existence of Freud and of Virginia Woolf and a book she ought by now to have read called *Women in Love* and a poet called T.S. Eliot who wrote very important poems that had strange titles and who said that mankind cannot bear very much reality, and that he had measured out his life with coffee spoons and that April was the cruellest month. She kept her bewilderment to herself. Life with Arnold Geddes had taught her how to hide deficiencies. But if she could not recognize and appreciate the intellectual delights, she could and did catch and savour the sheer vitality of the man. She was enlivened, encouraged, flattered to be 'his girl', tagging along through the summer. And was taken aback, put down, to find that he was going away: 'Leaving tomorrow for France.' Half a dozen of them, he and some friends, going to get as far as the Adriatic – possibly even across to Greece if time and cash permitted. When would he be back? Ooh – next term, October. It was the end of June. Off he breezed.

She cautiously raised her head and found that she was not heart-broken – possibly a little bruised, and surely entitled to be aggrieved? But also, and undeniably, a little relieved – though of what, was not clear . . . And the rest of the summer turned out very nicely. The college term wound down in a leisurely fashion; she had passed the essential exams for the second year, and there was a sense of ease and relaxation, sunbathing in gossiping groups, playing tennis on the college hard courts, planning the holidays. During those, she went away twice, once to Wales, youth-hostelling, with eight chums from college, and the second time to Eastbourne to stay with one of the chums whose home was there. Both ventures were acceptable to Arnold, falling into the category of activities promoting healthy minds in healthy bodies and precluding transgressions with the opposite gender. In this he was mistaken, inasmuch as all the girls, including Connie, were busy about finding, keeping or changing boyfriends, and meeting with reasonable success. Connie held hands, got herself kissed, defended against intrusions up her skirt and too far within her blouse, and generally had a very satisfactory time, pursuing and pursued.

When she found herself based at Wickenwood, she managed to get out almost daily, going into Collingford to see old schoolmates, with whom she would swim in the municipal open-air pool, now again open post-war, or play tennis on the municipal courts, or go for walks along the valley, swopping gossip, or sit in one of the town's two cafés, spinning out a coffee over chat. Pubs and beer were of course quite out of the question there in Collingford, and neither she nor her peers were in the least tempted to try those bounds. They were content with the status quo – provincial, English, conformist status quo circa late 1940s.

Back at college October arrived, but not Oliver with it. He had, it seemed, dropped off the edge of the world. Did she miss him? Seemingly not.

The Union dances got under way for the winter; Connie ran with the pack, busy with friends, boyfriends, hair-styles, and cobbling up new outfits from cast-offs since clothing was still on coupons. More by good luck than good management, she also did just enough college work to keep herself out of trouble.

At Christmas she perforce accompanied her parents to the usual church social. She wore her red velvet frock with the white lace collar as requested by her mother, and prepared herself to be thoroughly bored, which she was. Irritatingly, a young man with a boy-scout hair-cut and a Christian Endeavour badge in the lapel of his navy-blue three-piece pressed attentions on her and vastly increased her boredom, which she made no effort to conceal. Her father steered her into the corridor and left her in no doubt as to his requirements. That, he told her, was Edwin Bostock, the son of a colleague and client of considerable importance to the business. Her attitude was disgraceful and degrading, to herself and to the Geddes name and she was to go back in there and mend matters at once and he would have more to say later when they got home. If Connie had imagined herself emancipated, she knew otherwise now, as she trailed back into the village hall and spent the next hour partnering Edwin Bostock in the Beetle Drive. Over the potted-meat sandwiches at supper she learned that Edwin Bostock was 'in sausages'. Had she been less subdued, she would have yelped with laughter.

Young Bostock, as Arnold Geddes now styled him, became the subject of contention between daughter and father. Young Bostock fancied his chances with Miss Connie Geddes and apparently Bostock Senior found the notion agreeable and appropriate. Arnold cautioned his daughter, reminding her of her filial duties and incidentally reminding her in whose hands the purse strings lay and that she was as yet under twenty-one. Connie, with ill grace, found herself obliged to put up with Young Bostock's company: a visit to the Rex Cinema, a walk on Sunday afternoon, a trip to Salisbury Cathedral, with high tea at the White Hart. It was all excruciating. At home she was sullen. She longed for the new term, and when it came fled gratefully away from the young man in sausages and back to the diversions of college life.

But that was not the end of Young Bostock. At Easter there was a great row at Wickenwood. Or rather, a tirade from Arnold Geddes, flaring 'dumb insolence' from Connie, and a hard slap across her face to correct it. Mrs Geddes ran, with little steps, short runs to and fro across the hall, saying 'Oh! Oh!' Connie gulped back tears and rage and pounded up the stairs slamming the door of her bedroom to which she had been consigned. But she kept the arrangement made by her father and went to supper at the Bostock family home. In another context it would have been simply a dull, dutiful evening, well intentioned on the part of the senior Bostocks who made Edwin's 'friend' totally welcome. And Edwin was his customary polite self and made no unseemly advances, exacting only a chaste 'goodnight' kiss by way of carnal knowledge. So, nothing to fume about. But Connie, beneath a flimsy veneer of courtesy, was fuming. The row had altered cases and the slap had propelled parent and child on to uncharted shores. So that when six months later the parent was delivered the news of the daughter's *fait accompli* marriage to Oliver Bruce, it could well be interpreted as the deliberated counter-slap, victory to Connie, vaunting liberation.

But it had not been like that at all. Oliver had reappeared one day that summer and laid claim to Connie's attention. And without protest, she gave it. Her friend Barbara said, 'I'd tell him to take a running jump!' and Connie was instantly on the defensive, exonerating him: 'Oh, he couldn't help it – it was all last minute, and he had to go really . . .' Her friend Jill said, 'Oh-ho – I see dishy Olly's back on the scene! Lover come back to m-e-e-e – eh?' and Connie was instantly vexed, swiftly denying anything of the sort. He was not 'like that'. He was a most intelligent man, they had interesting conversations, she loftily explained. Jill said, 'Coo-er!' and rolled her eyes, prancing off. Connie could not have accounted for either of her responses. She was distantly aware of having been agitated by Barbara's disrespectful comment – the image ridiculed him, and that disturbed her. As to Jill's suggestive suggestion, those sexual assumptions – well, to be sure, there had been kissing and fondling, had there not? But yet there had been less of any sexuality between them than she had shared with casual partners fox-trotting at a Union dance ... But there again, their relationship, hers and Oliver's, could not be said to be Platonic, could it? And, now resurrected, it was the mixture as before.

This time round, though, he was tense and intense. He had not been enjoying himself of late. In the year since he had vanished, he had clocked up two abortive demi-affairs; his closest friend had got himself married; his next closest friend was about to follow suit; the congenial household in the Earls Court basement had broken up; he was on his own in a bedsit with a gas-ring off the Cromwell Road.

He talked a lot, sifting and analysing what he thought might be his feelings, about Women, about Bourgeois Morality, about the institution known as Marriage. He did not so much address her as air his thoughts in her presence. Once or twice a week they would go to 'the pictures', and there he would sit with his arm around her and from time to time turn and deliver a kiss. There was something almost impersonal about his kisses, something experimental, speculative. But she did not attempt evasion. She lent herself without protest, unsure of her role, as he seemed to be; she went along with it, part confidante, part pupil, very small part girlfriend. It was rather as though for both of them the relationship ran on potential; as though just around the next corner purpose would be revealed and fulfilled.

The weeks passed. Oliver's second-best friend got married and Oliver was an usher in a Moss Bros suit and Connie, as his 'friend', was of the party which was large and merry and witty and smart, and like nothing Connie had ever seen. And soon Oliver was tense and intense again, and the talk was increasingly of sex, but in a spirit of intellectual inquiry – not in the least libidinous. He did use a four-letter word which Connie had only ever encountered written on public lavatory walls and which jolted her. But then this was a man, not a boy – this was a man, who had been in the war, in the army. And soon, she accepted his vocabulary without tremor; and felt herself thereby to have moved into maturity.

They were, she later supposed, roughly equal in disadvantage, each in the same state of elementary sexual angst on the afternoon he pushed her to the shabby divan in the bedsit and attempted coition, though equality had no place in her perceptions at the time. At the time, she was only aware of discomfort, disarray and a failure that rested with her.

He did not propose to her or speak of love – just, quite soon after the muddle on the divan, he was talking aloud to himself about marriage, and shortly aloud to her too, about filling in a form and buying a ring and finding a witness and a register office. There was little joy in evidence. And none the morning she tagged along to the register office. Bemused and uncertain, she emerged with a ring on her finger and a new name, and found that Oliver was ahead of her in doubt. Already examining his regrets.

No, there had been no deliberated counter-slap aimed at Arnold Geddes.

She failed her finals. Or rather, when the results came out, they were poor, and to qualify she must take one of the exams again. She never did.

*

'Con? Con! Where are you, Con?' Gledwyn thrust open her bedroom door. She was still sitting slumped on her bed. 'Where've you put my shirt. Good God, aren't you ready yet?' He was in his peevish vein.

'You might at least knock,' she said.

'Look here, I can't find that shirt. I thought you said you were going to leave it ready!'

'Keep your hair on.' She hauled herself upright. 'I'm just coming.'

The shirt was where she had said it was, on a hanger in his wardrobe. Wordless, she pointed it out. Gledwyn huffed and shuffled: 'Should've said! Been looking in the drawers – shirts customarily belong in drawers, not ward-robes ...' But Connie was already out of the room, returning to her own. He was aggrieved by the prospect of the afternoon and was responding with cussedness, strewing the way with emotional tin-tacks, as usual. Betty had once said to her that Gledwyn used helplessness like other people use aggression. That was after she had left him, and was the only hint of explanation or extenuation offered. Betty had never been one to defend her actions or to enlist allies.

IV

It had been Betty and only Betty who had kept contact with her in the years following the unblessed wedding, for Connie had been disowned by Wickenwood. That neither surprised her nor distressed her. Whatever it was she lacked in her new life, it was not her old home. No, she was not dismayed to be disowned by Wickenwood. Had she, though, been claimed, in London? Before she reached the street outside the register office, she saw herself as an encumbrance; it was clear that she was not a prize.

When she eventually returned to Wickenwood, it was without enthusiasm. By that time she was herself a parent; Malcolm was five and Rowan two. It seemed a lifetime ago that she had been Connie Geddes.

The dog was now a spaniel, called Rab, Bosun having died. Apart from that, nothing had altered, and, as before, Oliver got on splendidly with the dog, easily with Betty, indifferent well with Gledwyn and not at all with the Gothick Progenitor. Gwyneth Geddes was not at home. She was in hospital, making a halting recovery from a gallstone operation. That was how Connie came to be back in the fold. Betty had told her on the phone: 'She's pretty rough, I'm afraid.' And Connie could only agree that a visit was in order, and from that to reunion with Wickenwood was just a step, with a push from Betty who thought the interdict too stupid for words, anyway. Arnold was induced to deem a visit acceptable in the circumstances and graciously deigned to draw a veil over past offences.

The truth of the matter, obvious to Connie, was rather less edifying. In recent time Arnold's son-in-law had ascended the firmament. The bright spark was up there in the constellation, his light shining in the darkness even of deepest Wiltshire; and in Collingford some had mused,

'Isn't that the fellow the Geddes girl married a while back? Never see her about these days ...' And Arnold Geddes had come to see, with St Paul, that: 'We then that are strong ought to bear the infirmities of the weak ...' Arnold had always numbered himself among the strong. Now he felt the magnanimity of his position.

Connie had no yearning for forgiveness. She had no desire to be back in the parental fold, but what else could she do except submit? What startled her though was Oliver's inclination to count himself in. She was not convinced by his claim of concern for 'the poor old bag'. It was soon apparent to her that he had a fancy to collect vassalage from his old adversary – which he did, using intellectual agility, deft condescension, baroque humour and a ravishing relationship with Arnold's dog. Arnold was duly brought low. To his Collingford peers, though, he presented a picture of cordial equality shared with his illustrious son-in-law: 'Oliver was telling me, the other day ...' 'Oliver quite agreed with me ...' In practice, Arnold spent longer hours in his study when the Bruces came down. And Oliver soon tired of these trips and increasingly opted out. But the children had by then discovered the local riding-stables, the grounds and out-buildings at Wickenwood, the Mullen and other wonders to outweigh the constraints of the place; and then they met up with the Hennessey children at Collingford swimming-pool. Trips to Wickenwood were reckoned as 'Ace!' And Connie complied, carried on the tide of their delight, Malcolm's and Rowan's.

Rowan. Oh Rowan.

What's to be done? It can't be evaded. Motherhood.

Say something to her.

What though? What?

The Air Cadets' Brass Band was pumping out selections from *My Fair Lady*.

'I've grown accustomed to her face . . .'

Connie took a parting look at the one in the dressing-table mirror, and, abstracted, combed and smoothed her hair. Hair now quite grey and well in keeping with the faded features and the hatching lines. From the rear she looked younger, less old; she had seen so, angling a mirror to reflect the figure held in the long cheval glass. The hair at the back of her skull was still dark, still thick; the form beneath still spare, unencumbered by the soft flesh of the female frontage which by sneaking degrees subsided, spreading southwards. Well. Anno Domini. So be it. She strapped on her watch. Two-thirty. Time to round up Gledwyn.

He fussed and fumed. He was grumbling now, limping heavily round the side of the house: 'These blasted shoes! I knew I should have stayed in my slippers! People *do*, you know – people with injuries do! Well, I shan't hang about – I can tell you! Damn and blast the bloody Fair. Don't see why I've got to go, anyway!'

'You haven't.'

They moved from blue shadow to sunstruck gravel sweep. 'Phoof!' He mopped at his forehead with the large white handkerchief. 'Well, I shall just put in an appearance and then that's that – and straight back home!'

V

Home. Holmlea. A name she had intended to alter but never had, initially because she could not decide on an acceptable alternative. She'd have settled preferably for a number but only the old farm cottages in her village carried numbers; all other dwellings bore names: The Beeches, Little Acre, Orchard Cot, Meadow View and so on. Holmlea. Eventually she found it had ceased to irritate her. She had had a low irritation threshold in those days, the year she moved, left Twickenham. 1975.

In retrospect she recognized how fearful she had been, making the move. Frightened. At the time she had not recognized her fear as fear. She had seen herself as hassled, stretched to cope with circumstances, naturally irritable, with so much to sort out. All of which was true of course. But the gut emotion had been fear. And as imperceptible to her as to everyone else. She was acclaimed as 'sensible' and 'enterprising'. 'Oh well done, Connie! Fresh fields, eh? Well, London's fast turning into one almighty traffic jam – we quite envy you! Good decision!'

Decision!

Certainly not hers.

Along with the quarterly gas bill and a mail-shot offering cut-price loose-covers, a letter. A letter from Appleton and Company. Would she please make an early appointment? Matters arising from her late husband's estate. What on earth ...? God knows it took long enough to finalize – Oliver had died intestate and it took for ever, but it was at last wrapped up years ago by numerous grey men, including of course those at Appleton's, the accountants ...

Appleton the elder had in the interim died. Appleton the younger had the secretary bring in coffee, and then informed Connie that irregularities had come to light. The Inland Revenue was pressing for results. 'I'm afraid the hounds are at our heels, Mrs Bruce. Time is not on our side!'

'But ... but ... everything was tied up years ago! He's been dead seven years ...!'

Ah. But it seemed that Mr Bruce had not made matters quite plain. On several occasions. Relating to his investments.

'Investments?'

Some of the theatrical ventures.

'Theatrical ventures?'

Why yes. Dublin, Pont de Vaux ... She sat in a daze, the recital flowing on. Incomprehensible. She stared at him in trapped silence. Thunderstruck.

Foreign currency transactions. Certification. Secured loans. Interest. Failure to disclose. Punts, francs, sterling. Several thousand pounds. Well, somewhere between fifteen and twenty-two. The Inland Revenue figures suggested the latter, alas.

Theatrical ventures? Theatrical? Ought she to know? She did not know. For Oliver had never told her ... Even had she been able to speak, she would not have revealed her total ignorance. Though whom she was protecting was far from clear . . .

And of course as there were no alternative sources, it was unavoidable, that number 21 would have to be sold. 'Well, no, Mrs Bruce' – a quizzical glance at her – 'the house *is* the security. Here is your signature, November 1963 . . .'

From somewhere she found the means to say, 'Oh – yes!'

And indeed there was her signature. She had. She had signed something. She could almost remember. Oliver saying, 'Formality, Con. Appleton's wheeze. Spreads the benefits.' She had no more idea than usual as to what he was talking about, happy to remain in ignorance of accountancy and tax . . . Not this Mr Appleton. Appleton the elder. Dead. Like Oliver.

'. . . and thankfully, the property will realize considerably more than the present pressures demand. I've been looking into your position, Mrs Bruce, and it could be that this . . . upset will have its brighter side. If you were to settle for a smaller property further out of town you could in fact retain some capital to swell your pension.' He was closing the interview, tidying papers, stowing his fountain pen in his inside pocket. 'For those on fixed incomes like yourself, the recent oil crisis and hyper-inflation are bearing specially hard. This move could prove beneficial. I understand that your children are . . . er . . . on their own feet now, more or less? Living away? A bungalow, perhaps! Well, thank you for coming in so promptly, Mrs Bruce!' A bracing smile and strong shake of the hand. Pleased with her. She had made no fuss. He suggested Fox and Sons to handle the sale. Decent firm, reliable.

'Thank you,' she said. 'Yes. Thank you.'

Only when walking blindly away up the street had it come, the wave of rage. You *bastard*! You used me, and the house, Oliver – you manipulating bastard! The hounds are at our heels, are they? At *mine* – at *mine*! You double-dealing *bastard*!

Quantities of gin in the solitude of her kitchen had released more rage, then tears, then bad, defeating memories.

VI

'Oh, this will sell well and quickly, Mrs Bruce!' the young man from Fox and Sons assured her.

'I'd rather you didn't put a For Sale notice outside,' she told him.

'Oh.' He didn't like that. Well, he could lump it. 'If you insist of course, though it is our policy to –'

'I'd rather not. Thank you.' Why was she saying thank you so frequently? 'I have my reasons,' she said. One, at any rate. She would at least defer the day when the neighbours would have to know she was leaving. Defer it, until she had herself absorbed the shock, and equipped herself with a plausible representation of a woman who wanted a smaller house now that the children, etc., etc. The 'keen interest' promised by Fox and

Sons began to manifest itself. Sometimes the young man would do the tour. Sometimes their office would ring and ask her if today she would show the client round as Mr Dewhurst had a full schedule of other appointments. She would say yes, and always loathed it, even with the courteous ones, and particularly with the less-than-courteous ones: 'Well, we'd have *that* out for a start!' 'Wouldn't want the carpets, anyway – past their prime a bit, aren't they?' 'Poky sort of room. I suppose we could knock that wall out.' She had need of all her celebrated facial composure. Some would be in and out in ten minutes. Some would wander round half a day. Surveyors came climbing and prodding about. She learned of damp and dry-rot and faulty guttering at 21 and brick-work on the north side which needed extensive pointing. The weeks dragged by. She slept badly, ate little, smoked much, made herself wait till six o'clock before starting on the gin. It did not sell particularly well, nor quickly, though the sale when it came was to a chap who had barely put his head in any room. Quick, he was: 'Yes. This will do very well. We'd like to exchange as soon as possible. We want to be in by the end of the month.' 'Excellent!' said Fox and Sons. 'Splendid!' said Mr Appleton. But she had found nothing for herself meanwhile. She would have to store the furniture, and rent.

She rang Rowan. '. . . and I'll store the furniture and rent, while I keep looking. Though – I've been wondering – perhaps I'll rent permanently – upkeep and repairs someone else's responsibility. I don't know. What d'you think?'

'Well – whatever's best for you, Mum.' As little true interest as she had shown throughout. Understandable?

In her last year at Durham University, into a live-in relationship with a chap called Clive, maybe getting married. 'Well, we might. Just a Registry do, couple of friends for witnesses, no hassle.' And, anyway, they were toying with notions of emigrating or 'bombing off to Italy for a year' or something 'imaginative'. Little imagination left for Mother's passing problems.

Mac was in Paris on a six-month course. 'I'd take advice, Mum. Ask Appleton – renting puts the money in someone else's pocket. And Mum – sell as much furniture as you can do without – storage charges are horrendous! What? Yes – I'm fine! Listen, I'll ring next week, this time next week, OK? Take care!' He'd met a girl. 'Philippa. What's she like? Well – she's nice! Um, tallish. Brown hair. Nice looking, natch! . . . Mm? Doing a post-grad at the Sorbonne. Oh yes, bright all right!' So. Perhaps he too might soon be marrying . . .

The rented 'bijou flat' in Sheen cured her of the renting experience. She resumed the dreary trudge round the commuter belt, 'where the prices are more commensurate with your means, Mrs Bruce'. The properties were commensurate with nothing in Connie's heart, which week by week sank lower. Exhausted and bemused, she would head away from the wilderness of outer London's graceless sprawl and batter her way back to the bijou flat to drown the day's failures in more gin. She did see friends from time to time. She did have a few friends, but they were the friends she had known through Oliver, Oliver's friends. They were nice to her, invited her to supper and Sunday lunch occasionally. Sometimes she went, though increasingly with the sense of being that awkward creature, the Spare Woman, the left-over of a duo. When one of them now said to her: 'My cousin's just found a super little place down in Hampshire – cottage in its own orchard, got it for a song! Apparently there are still good pickings out there in the sticks – how does the idea grab you?' she instantly replied that it didn't really, all her friends lived in town, and that at forty-six she was anyway too old to take on a whole new life-style, and so on. But she did then find herself musing. She had lived her youth in the country . . . But it didn't appeal. Neither though did the suburbs. Wearily she flogged on. It was the secretary at Appleton's who came up with Gloucestershire. One of those chance connections: 'My aunt, she's moving north, getting on a bit and going to live with her friend in Cheshire. She wants a quick sale – it's small, of course – she's always been a spinster, on her own. But it's in good repair and it's cosy, and, well, I thought of you. It's worth a look?' Holmlea.

Standing there amongst the tipped furniture and boxes that first night she had wept, silent tears streaming. She couldn't tell why: whether she was sorry, whether she was glad, whether she was simply played out, falling to pieces with the stress and speed of the whole lousy experience, the details of which she had revealed to no one – no one, not even her children; perhaps specially not to them, Rowan and Mac. Hyper-inflation. That was the reason.

She had unpacked; she had bought picture-hooks and hung the Modigliani print and the Samuel Palmer. The man from next door across the field had very decently offered and helped to lug some of the heavier furniture; the doors were small and narrow and the sofa had been a brute. His wife had brought over coffee and cake to sustain them. A pleasant middle-aged pair who asked no questions and, having assisted, assured her she had only to ask and withdrew. There was a village store. Cirencester was within reasonable distance. She would find her bearings.

She had been there six days: 'It's Mother.' Gledwyn on the telephone. 'Well, Betty knows more about it. Here, I'll hand over. . .' Connie left within half-an-hour and drove fast to Salisbury, the Infirmary.

'It's difficult to predict, Mrs – er? Bruce,' the Sister told her. 'It was not a severe stroke, but there's the kidney problem of course and one can't predict.' She led off down the ward: 'We have her on a drip. Oh . . . er . . . she may not recognize you – she's under sedation, and then there was the stroke . . . Mrs Geddes! A visitor for you! Your daughter's here.' Sister placed a chair and left.

'Actually, I don't think she knew there was anyone there.'

Betty said, 'That's mostly the sedative, Con. She'll be more switched on tomorrow.' Betty, who had appeared at her elbow, bedside, and was now steering her back to the hospital car-park. 'Are you OK to drive? Sure? Right. See you back at Wickenwood.' For Betty was adamant. 'You're not driving back to Gloucestershire today. You're coming back with me, ducky! No debate. And then I'll fill you in about it all, and you can come and see her again tomorrow.'

She had stayed a week at Wickenwood. Never her favourite place, it was nevertheless an oasis thanks to Betty, who lent her clothes, fed and supported her, and without explanations seemed to intuit the miseries of the past few months; and now this. Somehow that week Connie even managed to laugh, with Betty. She hadn't laughed for a long time.

But at the hospital there was no laughter. She was watching her mother die. Impotent, dismayed, she watched the disintegration. 'Mother?' Once, just the once, there had been fleeting recognition, 'Connie?' and a weary frown; then a twitch of what might have been a smile had the muscles of her face been less impaired. After that, no recognition.

'She's been asking for something,' Sister told her, day five. 'There! She's doing it now!' They advanced down the ward towards the emaciated upraised arm, feebly, endlessly waving, summoning: '-ng'any -ng'any -ng'any . . .' The rasping, questing voice.

'What is it she's saying?' Sister wondered. 'What is it she wants?'

She had to wait for an answer. Connie swallowed hard before she could speak. 'Herself.' She swallowed again against tears. 'Gwennie. It's her name.'

'Oh.' Sister mustered her professional voice and said kindly and firmly: 'She isn't suffering, you know, Mrs Bruce. This sort of confusion follows from the condition, and the drugs of course. There's no . . . meaning there. She isn't in distress.'

Connie thought, 'Wrong, Sister.' But she said nothing, merely nodded. All through that visit the call went on. And on. Nurses came and put screens round the bed. Connie sat holding the other hand. Saliva dribbled from the calling mouth. Connie wiped with a tissue. 'Gwennie, Gwennie, Gwennie . . .' pleading and questing.

The next day she was still. Her eyes were open, the motionless mouth bluish.

'She took a turn for the worse in the night, Mrs Bruce. Perhaps your brother – I understand there's a brother? I think he should be told – if he would like to make a visit. . .?'

Gledwyn unwillingly came, along with Betty. Connie had called Wickenwood from the payphone in the corridor.

Gledwyn stood dumbly staring. 'Gled . . .?' Betty placed a chair for him. He appeared not to hear, didn't move. As they watched, a trickle of thin brown fluid slid from the patient's nostril. Her son turned and almost ran, out of the ward, escaping.

Mrs Geddes did not regain consciousness. She had, they were told next day, 'died peacefully' at three o'clock in the morning.

Connie stayed a further day at Wickenwood and then went home. 'No, I'd better go – electricians and things – I'd better go now. I'll come back on Wednesday. I shouldn't be away another week, you know?' Truth was, she needed now to be alone. Betty did not press. 'You'll overnight with us after the funeral? Look – come down on Tuesday, Con. Go to the funeral with us from here, eh? Don't flog yourself, darling – you look all in.'

There must have been sixty, seventy there at Dympton church. A lot of villagers, locals. Gwyneth Geddes had been a shy, unsure woman, rarely out and about. Only once, in the fifties, had she been prevailed upon to open the church fête; but she had been regarded with respect and the locals turned out. 'It's the end of an era for them,' Betty said. And added, 'And for us.' An observation which only yielded its full significance when three weeks later she left Gledwyn and Wickenwood.

Mac did not attend the funeral. He sent flowers Interflora from Paris. It was Assessment Week, and Connie told him not to absent himself on her account, it was unnecessary, out of proportion in the scheme of things. From north Wales, geriatric cousins sent wreaths. Attendant at the church were a few elderly acquaintances, the generation which still wore hats, the residue of Arnold Geddes's contemporaries. Betty's and Gledwyn's children were there: Stella, who had recently met her New Zealander; Roy, with Eithne, who was pregnant with their first. Rowan and Clive came down from Durham. And from Collingford, a dozen or so middle-generation, family friends through Betty, the Lyles, the Crawfords, the Kepstows, several couples. The Hennesseys. The Hennesseys brought with them Kit, and his new wife Nicola.

It had never occurred to Connie that she would that day be seeing the Hennesseys.

Staring blankly down on to the coffin of her mother, she had felt only the unwelcome presence, away to her left. Leaving the graveside, she had kept her head bent, her arm through her brother's. Driving away from Dympton in the limousine, she did not look back.

Of the three of them, Betty beside her, Gledwyn in front beside the driver, only Betty could have been at peace with herself. Service beyond the call of duty, freely and lightly given. Betty had warmed Gwennie's declining years with good fellowship and humour. Gwennie had learned to laugh a little and tentatively even to venture towards a notion of self-respect, under Betty's benevolent regime. Whatever filled Betty's mind as the fields flowed by could not be muddied with guilt. Gledwyn? Who knew what went on inside that head? Not Gledwyn for a start. Connie wondered if she would ever be able again to see him without the imprint of that perfidious flight from the ward. But could she claim superior conduct, honestly? Overall?

Back at Holmlea these past few days she had confronted the fact that she and her mother had shared nothing, ever. Kinship, of course; mere accident of birth. And a roof and a domestic routine for a score of years; but nothing more. Nothing of import, nothing of truth offered, either side. Where lay the fault? With Mother? With herself? Both? Neither? Just when it was all but over, Connie thought she had found something very like intimacy, a rapport, with the foundering, questing figure in the hospital bed. 'Gwennie, Gwennie, Gwennie . . .' But one week later beside the grave she had not even been able to give her mother a final few moments' decent attention. So much for the touching fantasy of eleventh-hour rapport! They knew each other not at all, mother and daughter. Each half guessed at truths about the other, but none were ever invited or proffered. Did it matter? Would life have been different or better, troubles shared? Would Mother have been less unhappy with her lot if she had been able to speak about her life with Arnold? Would Connie's life have felt less of a mess if she had been able to tell her mother about Oliver . . . and everything . . .? An academic question but one that seemed inescapable, and poignant, today.

The limousine geared down and conveyed them reverentially between the laurels towards the funeral baked-meats, for 'about thirty I expect', laid on by Betty.

It had been almost three o'clock before the last of them drifted away.

Betty shed her shoes and capsized into an armchair. Connie handed her a glass of wine. 'Thanks.'

Gledwyn had taken himself off into his study.

Connie picked up glasses and plates about the room.

'Leave 'em, darling!' said Betty. 'Have yourself a rest.'

Connie found a bottle of white with an inch or two left and poured herself a glass. She was restless, exhausted but overwound. She stood at the window, gulped wine, picked up a plate discarded on the sill, put it down, wandered to the fireplace.

'Curious occasions,' Betty mused. 'Nobody knows what to do – what faces they ought to be wearing, I suppose.' She pondered, sipped. 'Anyway,' she said, 'the alcohol takes care of that eventually. Racket like any old cocktail party once the vino hits the spot.'

'Fag?' Connie lit one for Betty, one for herself. Then she sat. They smoked, drank left-overs, spoke of this and that in a desultory way.

'Funny old buffer, isn't he?' Betty said. Mr Wetherall, a one-time colleague of Arnold's. 'Eighty-five if he's a day, supposed to be deaf but he was lapping up some risqué tale about a bishop with the best of them, no trouble!' She said, 'He fancied Gwennie, once upon a time, y'know.'

From the depths of her armchair, Connie said, 'I didn't.' In a while she said, 'And did she fancy him?'

'Mm? Oh – I sometimes thought so. But actually I

think it was more a case of fancying being fancied – if you follow?'

'Yes.'

'She wasn't indifferent, put it that way. Not that she'd have done anything to encourage it in a million years.'

'No,' said Connie.

Betty said, 'Clive seems a nice guy.' Her first view of Rowan's live-in lover.

'Yes,' said Connie. 'I don't know him. But yes, seems a nice guy.'

'And will they, d'you think? Get married?'

'Looks like it.'

'Mm.' Betty drained her glass. 'All a gamble, isn't it, marriage?'

'Yep,' said Connie. 'Roy and Eithne seem OK.'

'I reckon Roy's better off than he knows. She's an odd little number but true as steel. With a bit of luck and a strong following wind he might notice, learn to appreciate her one day.' Betty had long settled for philosophical resignation in regard to her son. She did not find him lovable but saw no reason to beat herself about it.

'When's it due?'

'September. She's big, isn't she? Or perhaps it's because she's small.'

'She looks very fit, anyway.'

'Oh yes. She's a health freak, like Roy.' She added, 'Unlike Roy, she doesn't bore on about it. Well, not much, anyway,' she laughed. She said, 'Kit Hennessey's got himself a smasher – whatsername? Nicola. Extraordinary bunch, the Hennesseys. All look like those improbable beings in glossy holiday brochures – sort of immutably sleek! Now *there's* a lady who knows what face she ought to wear at a funeral!' Betty gave a laugh, dry, though not harsh: 'The one she always wears, Mary Poppins with a touch of St Teresa . . .! What was it, that rubric of hers?'

'Positive Thinking.' Connie turned away, found another cigarette.

'Oh that's right – Positive Thinking! I seem to remember Oliver being hilarious about that – well, it's been a great preservative, I have to say, whatever its deficiencies as a creed . . .' She said, 'I could have done without *quite* such unremitting bounce at the graveside. Well, I expect you heard her? "Oh, she died *peacefully*. Such a blessing! And I simply rejoice that she had a full life and a peaceful death and I shall plant a rose for her, celebrate her"! Almost singing it, like Julie Andrews skipping over the hills . . .' Betty yawned, stretched, and hauled herself upright. 'Well,' she looked round the littered room, 'I s'pose we have to shift this lot . . .'

They cleared away, washed up, set the furniture back in place.

'I think I'll toddle up the Mullen,' Connie said.

'OK. See you later.'

Heavily she climbed the Mullen. Toxic. Every cell in her body, probably. Too much wine, too many cigarettes, too much adrenalin. Her mind sagged. Echoes of that other funeral, Oliver's funeral, flittered and whispered about her path.

Was there ever, ever to be anything in her life, that was just plain simple?

She sank against the bole of her tree. Kaput.

VII

Oliver. Among the stricken, shocked and tearful faces at that ghastly London crematorium, her own had been composed. Pale, and composed. It was assumed – she read it in people's eyes – that she was marvellously coping, flanked by two dazed children. No one there, there or anywhere, knew that the marriage had been on the rocks. That three days before his death Oliver and she had 'discussed' its formal end. In a restaurant.

Oliver liked restaurants. In restaurants he felt assured, secure. Unlike at home from which he was frequently absent – away from his family, from her. His favourite quotation came from Evelyn Waugh's *Decline and Fall*. It made him laugh a lot. It made everyone laugh when he delivered it. It made her laugh, the first few times. It was Captain Grimes' lament on the subject of marriage: 'Oh, why did nobody warn me? I should have been told . . . the hideous lights of home and the voices of children!' Roars of laughter. Unless you were his wife, in whom the truth had dawned. Work, it was, the rationale that kept him so much from home. The nature of the job. Off to Glasgow, off to Birmingham, kept in town: 'Late meeting – not worth getting back, early start tomorrow . . .' Staying overnight with the Pagets, the Harrisons, the Delawares. Better yet – to Paris, a piece on Samuel Beckett; to Dublin, a programme on O'Casey; to New

York to talk with people who had known Scott Fitzgerald ... And her place was naturally at home. With the hideous lights and the voices of children. 'And, anyway, for God's sake, Con – we can't afford it! Fares, hotels – you wouldn't qualify for expenses – you know that! And you know our financial position just as well as I do!' She hadn't of course, as it turned out.

Yes. He liked restaurants. In restaurants you paid the piper, called the tune. You settled the bill and walked away; the timing was in your hands, and the options for emotional scenes limited. She had dripped her tears into the sole meunière, head well down. Other diners glanced and looked away. The waiter kept his eyes averted. Oliver talked on, solemn, excited. 'This is the most truthful thing we have ever done, Con. Overdue. For both of us.'

It was not a matter of other women, or other men, extra-marital affairs. Did Oliver have any? Depends what you mean by 'affair'. But brinkmanship, oh yes. Plenty of that. Heavy involvements with female colleagues, wives and daughters of friends. Seductions. Unto and into bed? Possibly. Irrelevant, anyway. For the emotional energy went elsewhere, extra-marital. Perhaps it occasionally extended to bed work. But that was, truly, an irrelevance. As was her own seedy affair. Had it qualified as an affair, that ignominious muddle? Well. Whatever it was, it had been extra-marital. And served to hang a divorce upon. Though they both knew that this débâcle at the restaurant table had nothing to do with other men, other women. This débâcle was on its way long before she met Alec Hennessey. It had been on its way for nineteen years, since the registrar had benignly nodded, and pronounced them man and wife . . . For what, then, was she weeping, bowed beneath his valediction?

'You can have the house of course, house and contents, and split down the middle whatever's in the bank when the case comes up. That's fair. Maintenance for the kids until they reach their majorities. Appleton will sort it out with the solicitor.' He had an appointment with a solicitor – one known to be well versed in handling divorces; they were to meet next week. The solicitor would advise as to the best approach – her adultery was of course the main plank, but the fact that several years had since elapsed could raise problems; but something would be worked out . . . He talked on. He could have been reviewing proposals for an extension to the loft. He showed no recognition of her distress. '. . . and access to the kids is obviously no problem – they can fly out in their holidays, I'll be settled in soon – and they're plenty old enough . . .' For he had signed a three-year contract with an American radio network, going to set up an Arts programme for them. Fait accompli. Well, there was nothing to consult *about*, was there? Nothing to discuss. He waved a dismissive hand, denying access to doubt. This was the obvious and propitious moment to get things sorted. Things, he said, had been mouldering too long already, and now as he was moving to the States here was the ideal opportunity! He was quite perky. He ordered more wine. And some pudding.

Yes, this débâcle had been on its way since day one.

It foundered, pipped at the post. He died. The world continued to believe in the Bruces' Happy Family.

Doug Delaware, his squash pal, came to see her some

weeks later: 'I haven't known whether to say this, Con –
I don't know whether it will help – but he was happy
when he died. He was happy that evening . . . Not feeling
off-colour or low or anything . . .'

'Oh. Thank you.' A wan smile, signifying gratitude.
Why disabuse him? Nice, decent Dougie Delaware.

'It's the most rotten unfair thing, just when everything
he'd worked for was within reach . . .' He was wretched
for her. 'Just when you were off together to the States
and everything. Life's a bitch, Con.' He told her that
everyone thought she was bloody marvellous, the way
she was coping. 'Well, I just wanted you to know . . .'

VIII

She had not been in love with Alec. She had drifted,
colluding in the flirtation on offer since that first
evening, as guests, Oliver Bruce and his wife at the Hennesseys' table.

She had had other offers before that – they appeared to
be part and parcel of the social round in Oliver's circle.
Oliver was not averse to men admiring his wife. Perhaps
it did something for his masculinity. It flattered him.
Once, quite early in their marriage, she had told him: she
had been propositioned. They had been at some dinner
do in town, a party for someone at the Beeb. Driving
home to 21 she had told him: the urbane and personable
Giles Macaulay had asked her to meet him. He had said

many beguiling things, including that he was more than half in love with her: 'He wants to take me to bed!' Oliver had given the news momentary consideration. 'How very flattering!' he said, agreeably. If she had meant to arouse dismay, proprietorial concern, awareness of herself as sexually desirable, she had failed. And then, it was several days before she saw and absorbed the extent of refined insult implicit in his reply. Whichever way you looked at it.

Later came Alec. But not, not love. She had drifted into collusion with Alec. It was easy, very easy. In those early sixties the children were enthusiastic for everything that Wickenwood had to offer and Twickenham could not supply; both of them were starry-eyed about ponies, as were Kit and Rachel Hennessey. And when these four were not together riding or 'helping' at the stables, they were together elsewhere. They were Best Friends. Alec was charming. He was good with children, would do anything, go anywhere. Picnics, rowing on the river, making dens, snowballing, swimming. Connie and Alec taking them about, weekends, not just school holidays now. Elinor? A peripheral figure, ever engaged in her own pursuits with her wide circle of busy friends.

Drifting was easy. Connie fancied being fancied. Like Gwennie. But unlike Gwennie, she had given encouragement. She was thirty-four, she was restless, she was vaguely on the market, gingered up by male admiration. 'All aboard for Wickenwood!' gunning the car out of London, eager children in the back seat, the car radio bashing out the Beatles: Love Me Do.

IX

Flirtation. Smiles, glances, innuendoes, shared cigarettes, a touch held longer than need be in support across a stream, over a stile. Delightful, being fancied.

And then one day, a kiss.

'I'm in love with you, Connie. I love you!'

'Oh.'

That was all she could find to say. Jolted from agreeable drift. She had not known what to do. And to add to confusion, she had not much liked the kiss. It was – wettish. In the charged split second, split attention: the unnerving declaration? the kiss itself? its unwelcome consistency? which? – which component fazed her most? And all she could muster was: 'Oh.'

Alec found that adorable. He had softly laughed, nuzzled her. 'You are wonderful, Connie! You're like no woman I've ever met – when they made you they threw away the mould!' And another kiss . . .

And then the children hove into earshot, running back through the wood.

The crucial moment had passed. In hindsight she saw it as crucial, that first of many moments at which she could have stepped back, extricated herself. And didn't. Twenty-twenty vision, hindsight. She was not in love with him. Was she hooked on admiration? Even twenty-twenty vision had never clarified precisely why she continued to drift. Vanity came into it; vacuity too. And drifting was easy: the frame was set and beset with happy children and a rolling routine to carry her on. And he was persistent. And she – what was she to say? How do you reject the man you have for months been mooning with, encouraging? For there was the nub. She had unquestionably invited a declaration. And the kiss.

And, it seemed, the bedding.

Well, what had she expected? What had she thought was in prospect as she smiled and glimmered and sucked shared cigarettes and answered warmth for warmth, pressing hands? She had not thought at all. Vacuous. Like a juvenile schoolgirl flexing her charms with a handsome boy on the school bus.

'I'm in love with you, Connie.'

Not on the school bus. Two fully fledged adults, chronologically speaking.

'Oh, Connie! My God – I want you! We must find ourselves a bed . . .!'

'But . . . I'm married! You're married . . .' Unemphatic, shifty, drifting.

'Oh, *Connie*!' A heavy kiss, kissing away the irrelevance.

And indeed, it was more than a little late to be summoning social mores. They had always been there, Oliver and Elinor. Their existence had been no deterrent. Had Oliver's existence supplied some seminal stimulus, even? She was angry with Oliver, had for years been resentful. Elinor? Well, Elinor, inasmuch as Elinor figured in Connie's imperfect grasp of the situation, Elinor remained the smug nonentity written off by Oliver. She had no care for Elinor, did not like or respect her. Alec never mentioned her. On the rare occasions when their three paths briefly crossed, Alec showed no discomfiture; and Connie found in herself a talent for dissimulation as spontaneous as Alec's.

And the children? Were happy and busy. And this . . . this . . . whatever it was in which she and Alec were engaged – it had nothing to do with them, did it? The rolling routine rolled on.

It took place in London, the bedding.

Alec was in town for a conference. Oliver was abroad for a week.

What was she up to, scurrying to their rendezvous that evening? Why go at all? Just the drift gathering momentum? Or was she purposeful, in search of the Great Experience which would put an end to weightlessness, confirm her in the league of lovable women?

Not in his conference hotel of course. In a pretty insalubrious one in some backwater, 'Mr and Mrs Smith' in the register under the single light-bulb.

'Darling, darling! Oh, Connie! Oh, oh, OH . . .'

So. Some sort of affirmative experience for him, then. Not, in the event, for her. Her preoccupation throughout had been with the efficacy of the old dutch cap which three hours ago at home she had wrestled into place.

'Oh you're beautiful, Connie. Beautiful . . .!'

'I must go. No, I have to get back – the baby-sitter . . .'

'Go? Darling! No. Not yet . . .'

'I must, I really must!'

He rang the next day, for more.

She prevaricated. Baby-sitter, she couldn't get a baby-sitter, as indeed she possibly couldn't; but it was prevarication.

'Aah – *hell*!' Desolated. 'It was wonderful, darling . . .!'

'Yes.' She had to say something. It could only be 'Yes'. She caught sight of herself in the hall mirror, and turned away. 'Look, Alec, I have to go now. Got to fetch the kids . . .'

'Soon, Connie. Soon again! When'll you be down at Wickenwood?'

'Oh. Next month, I suppose.'

'Well, yes, but *when*?'

'I don't know. School holidays – we're going away, I think.' They were. They were going to Devon, to Oliver's parents' home near Kingsbridge, for a fortnight this time, not the customary week. 'Dad pressed,' said Oliver with resignation. 'Well, what can you say? I guess we owe it to them. It's only once a year . . .' But all this belonged in a separate compartment within Connie. In speech with Alec she found herself shying from uttering Oliver's name. While at the same time having a sketchy notion that if she did, Alec would not share her discomfort: he would possibly even ask warmly after him with the ubiquitous charm he freely dispensed. 'How *is* he, dear old Oliver?' An unprepossessing notion, it lay with much else, neglected silt beneath the drift. 'I'll be down for the Fair anyway . . .'

'That's a month away!' he said.

'Yes . . . well, look, Alec, I must fly – the kids'll be waiting! See you then, OK? Bye!'

Thoughts bobbed and bumped about her mind as she handled the car, gear up, gear down, along the school run. Thoughts, but without thought. The images were present, rambling incoherently about. No energizing act of thinking harnessed them to judgement. Images aplenty – herself with Alec in a bed; herself delivering coffee to Oliver at his typewriter, lighting a cigarette from his and lending an attentive and appreciative ear as he read out a paragraph, testing it for intelligibility; Tamzin Barker who was coming to tea from school with Rowan today and who couldn't eat dairy products; the suitcase in the loft, for Devon; herself in a chemist's she found outside their locality, buying a tube of spermicidal jelly; the list in her handbag of things to get before Devon, new swimming-trunks for Mac – Marks and Sparks would be the place, and new pyjams for Rowan there too; the spinach she'd washed and put in a bag in the fridge, to go with her poached egg tonight; Wickenwood's telephone number which she *must* ring tonight too, overdue duty call to Mother; herself with a flock of kids, her own and Hennesseys' in Collingford, Alec in the grocer's picking up something for Elinor; the narrow twin beds in which she and Oliver would pass the nights at his parents' home; the sitting-room there, its three-piece suite and its tiled fireplace and tiled mantelshelf topped with brass ornaments and the photograph of Oliver aged eighteen, close-cropped new recruit in army uniform, a child; Mac's school satchel with the broken strap which must be repaired, taken to the cobbler's sometime in the holidays . . .

'Mummy, Miss Steading said you've got to sign this and I've got to give it in tomorrow and then I can bring it home again.' Rowan, waving her end-of-term report.

'Oh – OK. Hello, Tamzin! Jump in. Mind your fingers!' Doors closed and off to Mac's school, images receding; and those inviting judgement, sinking back into the silt.

X

A few nights later she woke in the small hours to a sense of intention, a lift in spirit: a disinclination to pursue the course with Alec any further. And a tendresse, a wish to protect the union of her marriage, hers and Oliver's. They had been together a long time. She heard his steady breathing beside her in the dark. She had not heard his late return. But here he was. And along the landing, the two more people, the two they had together made, despite everything.

She thought of Kingsbridge, the coming visit to Austin and Dorothy; she thought of the generosity and graceful tact with which she had been accepted, the sudden bride. She thought of those early days, she and Oliver tramping round in search of living quarters, the tatty furnished rooms, the grime and grease of departed tenants; the Picasso print they'd pinned on the bedsitter wall, and later over the fireplace in the first proper flat, furnished with offerings from Austin and Dorothy: a hand-me-down sideboard; a fumed-oak chest of drawers; and, brand new, two Lloyd-loom basket chairs, which they had painted gloss white, she and Oliver, one Sunday morning, unable to bear the bilious 'beige' any longer, and hoping that the parents would never get to know because their feelings might be hurt; and it was all right, because they never did. The chairs had done sterling service over the years. One, which had been left out in the rain in the children's den behind the garage, never quite recovered and departed in a blaze of glory on last year's Guy Fawkes bonfire; the other survived yet: repainted, it stood in Rowan's bedroom now ...

Oliver sighed, stirred in his sleep and settled again. She had packed a few things for the holiday already. Mac's new swimming-trunks – he'd grown two sizes in one year ... Did Oliver still have some wearable bathers? Must check up – days on the beach ...

Calm, and peaceably grateful next to her husband, she slept again.

XI

The senior Bruces had migrated south when Austin reached retirement. Their detached chalet bungalow stood with others, their gardens bordering the estuary waters. On the first visit half a dozen years ago Oliver had told his parents, 'Splendid! Lovely, lovely! Marvellous situation. Yes, *very* comfortable! Charming!' *Sotto voce* in the bedroom later, he said to Connie, 'They've achieved a miracle! Suburban Birmingham retained intact in the face of Mother Nature's best efforts!' And they had smothered laughter together, enjoying the easy intimacy of flippant ridicule. It was, she came to realize, the most accessible form of intimacy that they possessed. And it served, of course, to buoy them through the longueurs of statutory annual visits. This one, though, was going quite well.

They did the rounds, made the trips: a day on Dartmoor; a day at Slapton Sands, the adults in anoraks the children in swim-suits and goose-pimples; the cliff-walk at Start Point, granny staying in the car, lunch at a Salcombe hotel; the cruise on the River Dart. The nice retired people from next door came in to renew acquaintance with Oliver Bruce over six o'clock sherries, and the next day granny baby-sat while grandpa took his illustrious son and his daughter-in-law to post-prandial drinks with some very nice people in the third bungalow along.

Austin was proud of his son. He relished his company, giving and getting mental stimulus notably missing in retirement with his wife. Whether Dorothy was proud of her son was not clear. She would say to her grandchildren, 'You must be very proud of your clever Daddy!' and they would grin and giggle and oblige: 'Yes!' But her interests and energies were otherwise directed towards whether the car window should be closed against the possibility of someone getting neuralgia, or whether there would be enough hot water for two baths, whether everyone had noticed those beautiful tints in the view just now, whether Austin ought not to get an electric lawn-mower instead of having to heave that heavy old thing round what with his rheumatism, and whether the children realized that if they didn't eat their crusts up their hair would never curl. Dorothy was by no means a shrinking violet; she had plenty to say, but it could not be classified as stimulating. Over recent years Austin had developed certain tics, testimony to irritation under wraps; seated in the armchair, his fingers would twitch and prod along the moquette, his foot tap the fitted carpet; a high, sharp, mirthless laugh would presage expostulations directed at his chattering wife. 'Now, now, Dorothea! You've told them that already!' And in his braces, doing his morning chores, clearing the fireplace or the pedal-bin, he would whistle between his teeth, an angry travesty of cheeriness, shoulders tensed.

'Like escaping carbon monoxide, poor old bugger,' Oliver said to Connie. 'How the hell he tolerates her . . .' He shook his head, sombre with sympathy. It was a reading of the situation accepted by Connie. But one which she would soon begin to question to herself. Maybe Austin was not the only victim in that union. Austin was not without blemish. She would begin soon to identify the Bruce arrogance – the flair, with no tenderness. And to see Dorothy in a new perspective, the fugitive finding haven in obtusity.

Connie went down the sloping lawn to call the children in to supper. Chill, drizzly mist had curtailed the day out and Oliver had taken them to buy shrimping nets in Kingsbridge, with which, clad in anoraks and wellingtons, they scooped half-heartedly at the ebbing waters. 'Any luck?' she asked them.

'It's jolly smelly.' Mac was bored.

'There aren't any shrimps here, anyway,' Rowan said. 'Shrimps live in pools.'

'Well, never mind! Supper's almost ready – c'mon – and the sun's going to shine tomorrow. Daddy and grandpa are taking us for a day at Brixham. Lots to do in Brixham!'

'What's at Brixham?'

'Oh, lots of fishing boats – and things. Come on.'

Trudging up the lawn, Rowan drooped: 'Mummy, is it pilchards again?'

It was, as a matter of fact. Connie had just come from the kitchen, which nightly provided a high tea of lettuce, tomatoes, radishes, Heinz mayonnaise, and either slices of a ham-like substance or tinned pilchards. 'Wait and see.'

'Ugh, I hate pilchards!'

'Sssh! Well, I'll do you an egg . . .'

'Can I have egg too?' said Mac.

'Yes. Now, leave those in the porch and go and wash!'

Dorothy wagged her head across the table: 'Tst, tst!' she said. 'Fish makes you brainy, you know! Faddy-fads! Never be brainy if you won't eat fish!'

The sharp, barking non-laugh from Austin: 'Now now, Dorothea! Let them be, let them be!' He took a sip of orange squash and said to Oliver: 'Early breakfast, leave at seven – we'll be in plenty of time – though I'm quite happy to take you to Exeter. Save messing about with connections!'

'No, no,' Oliver assured him. 'Torquay's fine. Don't want to interfere with the Brixham trip.'

Connie blinked. Anger and disbelief contended with grim recognition of the old familiar charade. He *couldn't* be – not *here*, not *now*. And he was, of course. Going.

Rueful, Oliver met her straight, fierce glance and shrugged, lamenting, 'Just had Josh on the phone. There's a flap on. Duty calls!'

The phone had not rung; the call had been initiated from this end – she knew, anyway, the time-honoured,

118

tried and tested means and methods. The familiar charade.

Dorothy was declaiming: 'Well, I think it's wrong. Funny lot they must be, expecting you to give up your holiday. They know it's your holiday! That's not right!'

'You know nothing about it!' rapped Austin; no introductory non-laugh.

'I know as much about it as you!' she retorted. 'We all know it's his holiday!'

'It's all right, Mother,' Oliver soothed. 'These things happen, it's that kind of job . . .'

'Precisely!' said Austin.

'. . . and I'll be back in no time!' Oliver smiled warmly at his wife. 'I'm leaving the car,' he told her, in the manner of one making appropriate sacrifice, concerned for the common good, 'so you can all go ahead with the plans.' Austin's car was a Hillman Imp.

Connie was acutely aware of the arena and her place in it, the focus of all eyes, and, in particular, those of her children. 'Oh. Right – OK.' She made her mouth smile.

'There now. We shall get on splendidly, though it is unfortunate,' said Austin. 'A pity, but there!' He returned with deliberation to an earlier conversation with his son: 'I would never have associated Coleridge with educational theory, you know. But then I'd no idea he was a disciple of the German school. Kant, you were saying?'

'Kant specially, but Schelling too. Kant's theory of knowledge, and Schelling's *Naturphilosophie* – the "organic unity" idea. . .'

The rhubarb and custard came and went, the men talked on, absorbed. Connie and Dorothy cleared the table; the children went for a last canter in the garden; coffee was made. Connie avoided Oliver's eyes as she set it down in the sitting-room. She returned to the kitchen. 'Oh you go and sit down, dear!' said Dorothy at the washing-up. 'This won't take long, these few things!'

'Oh, no!' said Connie jollily. 'I'll just wipe up and then I'll get those two mudlarks into their baths!'

'Well, I put the immersion heater on at four – there'll be plenty of nice hot water! Mudlarks!' Dorothy laughed, equally jolly.

By the time Rowan was scrubbed and in her bunk and Mac was in his bath, a change of plan had occurred. Oliver, in his raincoat and armed with his hold-all, was leaving. He and Austin had agreed that the even better course was for Oliver to catch the night train up to Town. Obvious, wasn't it? Best all round! Oliver said cheerio to his daughter and to his son through the bathroom door. Austin, jingling his car keys, was ready to depart and wearing his trilby hat. Oliver kissed his wife's cheek: 'Back soon as poss, darling!' he squeezed her elbow, smiled. 'I'll phone.'

The sun did shine the next day, inaugurating a fine, hot spell. The Brixham visit was an average success, the children's interest sustained for an hour or so by the quay-side bustle of boats on twinkly water, and inspection of crabs and lobsters crouched captive in wicker traps. Mac wanted to know why those were called 'pots' but nobody had an answer. Rowan wanted to know if lobsters could hear but nobody knew that either. Both children viewed the victims with that equivocal eagerness composed of satisfaction and dismay: 'Oh, look at that *huge* one! Aaah, poor thing!' 'That one's waving!' 'It's not! It's eating something!' 'Yeough!' 'Mum – do lobsters and crabs like each other when they're in the sea?' 'Mummy, are those its eyes?' '*I* shan't ever eat one!' 'Ugh! Neither shall *I*!'

'Oh, but they're delicious!' Grandpa chuckled.

'Eeeoooh, *Grandpa*!'

Connie judged crustaceans to have passed their peak in interest value: 'Hey – look, those fishermen are making ready. Let's go and watch them cast off!' Ice-creams were consumed at a table on the pavement outside a café. Granny took off her cardigan and announced that she would wear her straw hat tomorrow if this went on. She was smiley today, had less to say, was more – tranquil. They all were. It must be the weather. Austin called Dorothy 'pet' at one point, and she took his arm along the waterfront. Furthermore, when the children asked for fish and chips in newspaper, the intended luncheon in an hotel was lightly abandoned and astonishingly there they all were sitting on a bench, eating fish and chips with their fingers, and when Granny leant across and said to Rowan, 'I thought you didn't like fish!' she was smiling and Rowan giggled comfortably: 'I like fish like *this*!' and Austin had not sought to restrain 'Dorothea'. And then after they had wiped their greasy fingers and put their papers in a litter bin, the children said they wished they could go to a beach now; the Brixham agenda was cheerfully discarded and off they drove to find one. Mac bathed in his underpants and Rowan in her knickers since swimming-gear was not on board, though happily a couple of towels were found still in the boot. Austin removed his shoes and socks, rolled up his trousers, and, in shirt-sleeves and braces, paddled.

Connie rolled up her jeans and paddled too. She stood, head back, eyes closed against the sun, silky water caressing, rising and falling against bare flesh and with a sudden uprush of fervour, almost frenzied, longed to be headlong awash and naked in the wide, rolling waters; for a moment she was caught up in a kind of physical necessity that for sure could not be answered. And entangled in the need and the frustration was the image of departure, displacement as the primary implacable force in charge of existence, and a vivid immediate moment's rage with her marriage, the man and his priorities, her incompetence, and his.

And then the moment had gone, and there she was, waving to Rowan, smiling and trudging through warm crunchy sand to join Dorothy, propped peacefully against a dune. 'You must bring your swimsuit tomorrow,' said she. 'If it's going to stay like this a beach is the best place to be, eh?'

'Absolutely!' said Connie.

So that's what they did for the following days: they packed ample picnics, took deckchairs and paperbacks and a couple of umbrellas for shade and surrendered themselves to salt-sea and heatwave and the pervading fragrance of Ambre Solaire. 'Positively French Riviera!' said Austin, lighting his pipe and going for another paddle.

*

Oliver rang the first evening. 'How's it going?'

'Very well,' said Connie. 'We did Brixham and then went on to Slapton. Fabulous weather.'

'Good, good! Stinking hot in this filthy city!'

'Yes, it must be.'

'Look. I'm not sure how long this is going on – you know how it is. Lempton was supposed to show up but didn't. Anyway, I'll be back as soon as possible. Could use a beach, not half!'

'Yes.'

'I'll ring again. Oh – Gary and Jan send love. Keep the aspidistra flying!'

'Your father'd like a word.'

'Oh – right.'

She left them to it. 'He's not sure,' she told Dorothy. 'He says it's horribly hot and sticky in town.'

'Hmm,' said Dorothy.

Oliver rang again on the fourth evening. 'How's things?'

'Wonderful!' said Connie. 'We're having a splendid time. And we're just working our way through a bottle of Moselle.'

'Are you, by Jove!' As startled as she intended him to be. Very satisfactory. Slightly tiddly, she was enjoying the moment.

'Uh-huh. More in the fridge, just supposing we're awake enough to crack it.'

'Hey! Get *you*!' He was off balance. 'Mother too?'

'Oh yes. You bet!'

'Well, well! You're obviously an enlightening influence!'

'We're having a good time,' she said. She did not ask the question. She didn't say, 'When will you be back?'

'Well, look,' he said, 'I think there's progress this end . . .'

'Uh-huh.'

'Couple of days might see it off.'

'Oh, right.'

'Well, talk to you soon.'

'Yup.'

'Bye for now, then!'

'Byeee!'

Rowan and Mac were at the kitchen table, writing postcards to friends. She did not tonight fabricate for them love from Daddy that he had not sent. Neither of them appeared to be noticing one way or another. 'Mummy, *is* there a hyphen in sun-tan?'

The next morning Connie went off in her self-appointed role as shopper for the day's picnic. Kingsbridge had lately sprouted a delicatessen; Austin, on his insistence, provided the money. On her way back she passed the boutique which Kingsbridge had recently also sprouted. She slowed by the window again, hesitated, and then went in. It fitted. As though it had been made for her. White piqué, well cut, beautifully finished. 'Oh that does look good!' said the proprietress, and she was right. The halter neckline, the scooped low back, small waist above slender hips and belling hem-line; and all that glowing nut-brown skin . . . There were rope-soled canvas espadrilles with laces to criss-cross up your ankles, in vibrant colours. She chose emerald. She wrote out the cheque with satisfaction enhanced by total absence of the usual guilt. She hummed to herself, swinging Dorothy's shopping-bag and the big shiny black carrier from the boutique. She had bought it for no other reason than that she fancied it – not for the sake of presentability for some occasion or other, not because she needed it. Just because she wanted it.

She wore it that evening. 'Oooh, Mummy!' said Rowan.

'Que madame est très belle! Très chic et très belle!' cried Austin, and bowed with the old-world gallantry with which he showed his affection for his daughter-in-law. 'You look like something out of *Vogue*, my dear!'

'Nice, isn't it?' grinned Connie. 'Not exactly practical but –'

'It's very pretty, dear,' said Dorothy, 'very posh!'

'Is it for the beach?' said Mac and flushed when everyone laughed, but Connie said, 'Well, you're right in a way – it's called a sun-dress, but I think it's a bit – posh – for the kind of things we do at the beach!'

They all went for a riverside walk after supper. 'If you would do me the honour?' said Austin, proffering his arm to Connie and raising his panama. Laughing, they strolled on. Mac took some photographs with Grandpa's Kodak. 'I don't think the light's really good enough,' he said, but clicked away at boats and ducks. 'You should take one of your glamorous mother!' said Austin, and Connie was placed in a pool of slanting light between the trees, and Mac officiated. Winding the film on, he shyly murmured to her, 'You do look nice, Mum!'

'I hope the sea doesn't come in too much,' said Rowan

anxiously as they headed back for bedtimes. She and Mac
had built a magnificent sand boat which you could sit in.
Plans for tomorrow's refinements were in hand; more
shells and stones for decoration, of course, but also
Grandpa had an old wheel from a garden barrow, in the
garage it was, and he said that yes of course they could
have it, use it for the steering-wheel. He now assured his
grandchildren that the boat was well above the tide-line
and that Rowan need not worry.

When they got back, the gate was ajar. On the garden
bench sat Oliver.

'Good gracious!' Austin sped forward. 'My dear boy!
How did you get here? How long have you – ? We've
been for a walk! Oh, you should have telephoned, I
would have collected you! Taxi? Great Scott, lad! Well,
well – anyhow it's good to see you. How very nice.'

'Daddy!' Rowan trotted up.

'Hello, Dad!' said Mac.

'You'll have had your supper,' his mother supposed.
'You weren't expected,' she told him.

'I had something on the train – buffet. Hello, darling!'
he leant and kissed Connie.

'Hello.'

'You look terrific!'

'Doesn't she?' said Austin happily. 'Well, come on,
come on. Let's not all stand round here. Goodness! *What*
a nice surprise!' He took up the hold-all and bustled
ahead with his latch-key.

Indoors Oliver produced a carrier-bag. He brought
forth a bottle of Bristol Cream and presented it to his

father, who protested that there was 'no need for that, son!' but was obviously pleased. For his mother there was a phial of Yardley's Lavender Water. She glanced at it. 'Thank you,' she said, setting it aside. For Mac, the *Observer's Book of Aircraft*: 'Ooh, thanks, Dad!' For Rowan, the *Observer's Book of Horses and Ponies*: '*Oooh, Daddy*! Thank you – it's the one Tamzin wants! Oh, goody!' And for Connie, a silk wrap, Italian, sumptuous, vibrant deep blue shot with sea-deep green. 'Put it on,' he said.

'It goes with your espadrilles!' cried Rowan.

'My, my!' beamed Austin.

'Thank you,' said Connie. Oliver lightly kissed her. 'Suits you,' he said, and imparted a hug. He opened his hold-all: 'And these – for all of us!' Two bottles of vintage claret. 'I gather you've all been bibbing!' He grinned at his father. He tossed the tissue paper into the coal scuttle and clapped his hands. 'Glasses!' he cried. 'No need for this to be chilled – indeed, that would be vandalism! Room temperature for this!' and as Austin brought four glasses from the sideboard, 'Six, Dad!' said Oliver, and Austin complied, with a roguish, 'Oh-ho – my word!' 'Corkscrew?' said Oliver. He bent to his purpose with concentration. Slow and steady, he drew the cork and gently sniffed at it, and then at the wine: 'Hmmm. Now this,' he said, carefully pouring, 'is ra-a-a-ther special.' He handed round the glasses, raised his own: 'Cheers!' he said. 'Cheers!' they all replied, and sipped.

Austin said, 'Oh, hmmm! *Very* nice!'

Dorothy said, 'I like that white one better. The one we've been having.' She critically eyed her glass.

'Come, come, Dorothea! You're being introduced to the real McCoy here!' Austin cried, jovial and irritated. And then hastened to add loudly, 'Not that the Moselle was anything but perfect!' He merrily raised his glass to Connie.

'It's sour!' Rowan drew back from her sip, and Mac pursed his mouth.

Austin laughed, 'Well, well, it's an acquired taste! But this is the real McCoy! One day you'll appreciate such things, eh?'

'They have vulgar appetites,' Oliver disposed of that and stretched himself in an armchair. Austin, chuckling in approval of the wine and the witticism, settled in the other. 'So, here we are, all together again! How very very nice! You managed to sort out the problem, then!'

'Yes – yes, eventually. It *was* the new chap – absurd appointment, job should have been Gleeson's by any criteria, but internal politics being what they are at the moment . . .' – Austin listened with attention as the tale unfolded – '. . . anyone with experience would have understood the implications . . . *amour propre* rather than contractual minutiae . . . can't muck around with that bunch – too much clout . . . technical boys pulling the plug . . .' – he refilled his glass, topped up his father's – '. . . studio time . . . throwing their weight about . . .'

Dorothy had taken herself off somewhere. Connie murmured to the children, 'C'mon, time for bed.' Oliver patted Rowan as he talked on, receiving her goodnight kiss and Mac's departing wave. Connie took her time. The children had no need of supervision. She dawdled in the bedroom, folding things. When they were in bed, she wandered out into the dusk. Dorothy was idly dead-heading such spent blooms as were revealed by light from the windows.

'All tucked up?' she said.

'Hmm.'

They stood together above the softly slapping waters. Dorothy said, 'Weather's on the turn. Could thunder for two pins.'

'Hmm, 'tis close.'

'Well he's missed his holiday,' said Dorothy.

Connie did not reply.

'D'you know what I'd like?' said Dorothy.

'What?'

'I'd like a nice big glass of that white wine! How about you?'

Together they giggled off up the garden. In the kitchen they sat drinking their nice big glasses of white wine, and talking domestic nothings. Footsteps, and Oliver appeared en route to the cloakroom. 'What's this!' he bantered. 'Secrets?' He glanced at Connie.

'Hen-party,' his mother said tranquilly.

Moving on, Oliver said, 'Well come and be hens with us!'

'With the cocks,' said his mother, not moving; but her son had gone.

Austin put his head round the door: 'Girls! girls! There you are! Come and join us! Don't deprive us of your company, eh?' He was quite merry. Dorothy appeared to be about to say something, but didn't. Gathering up the Moselle bottle and balancing her glass, she launched off to the sitting-room, singing. She sang: 'Cock-a-doodledooo, my dame has lost her shoe, my master's lost his fiddling-stick and doesn't know what to dooo!'

But it was Austin who held Connie's attention, his face jolted by colliding emotions: distaste was there – and anger? Or was it contempt? Dismay, certainly; a pulse of apprehension, the orderly man confronted by capering caprice. Then, 'Dorothy!' He stepped after her, authoritative: '*Dorothy*! Lower your voice for goodness' sake, you'll waken the children!' But Dorothy paused only to free a hand and flick open the french window before capsizing slowly to the sofa, singing on. She sang again: 'And Master's lost his fiddling-stick and doesn't know what to doooo!'

Austin smartly clicked the french window shut: 'We don't want the moths in!'

'Oooh,' said Dorothy, 'don't we? I don't mind the moths. We don't mind a few old moths, do we? They can join the party, join the cocks and hens!'

Connie hovered, uncertain, in the doorway. Austin, frowning now, moved stiff and swift behind the sofa and whisked the silken blue wrap from the approach of his wife's subsiding shoulder. 'Oh, I know it's there,' said Dorothy evenly and without looking at her husband. 'I know where Connie's present from Oliver is. I shall not *lean* against it. I shall not spoil it. You need not fash yourself. Ah,' she said, acknowledging Oliver's reappearance, 'and here he is!' She smiled benignly.

Oliver flicked a glance at his father, dropped into an armchair and, pouring more claret, said to everyone and no one in particular, 'Any chance of a sandwich?'

'Oh yes,' said Dorothy. 'Good chance. All the usual

chances.' She did not stir; quite relaxed. 'You know where the bread-bin is, I expect.'

A dull flush mounted Austin's face, anger on the move; and Connie was suddenly animated, saying overly loud, 'There's the pan bagna left from lunch! Still in the cold-box! I could do with a bite myself – anyone else? Well I'll rustle up a trayful, eh? there's pâté too . . .' and bustling away to the kitchen. Crisis averted, something salvaged.

Who, or what? Who or what had she so pressingly needed to salvage? Austin's equilibrium? Dorothy's neck? The *bonhomie* of the past few days? Herself? Ah. She hated rows. Herself then, salvaged. She feared rows, confrontation. Over the years she'd picked up Brownie points for emollient skills: beatified, the peace-maker. But actually it was fear, not principle, at work.

Pâté, salami, slivers of ham, pan bagna . . . What else? Few tomatoes? She rinsed them under the tap. From behind her Oliver's presence arrived, one hand reaching to scoop salami, the other fondling across her sunbrowned back. Through his mouthful he said into her ear: 'What's going on in there, then? She boozed-up, or just bloody-minded?'

Flinching, Connie replied, 'Why either? Just pratting about a bit. Letting her hair down!' She moved from his hand, carried the tomatoes away to the tray. He followed, eating meat, and slid against her: 'You look good enough to eat yourself! Delectable . . .!' He sought and found her mouth and kissed it.

She looked at him without cordiality: 'Like the salami?' she said, drawing back.   He gave a yelp of laughter. 'Hey! Honeybun, honeybun . . . Hmmmm! Let your hair

131

down, let your hair down!' he whispered, roused and pressing. 'Whoof! Yes, yes!' he murmured, rammed against her.

Sounds of movement in the hall. Austin's footfall?

'*Shit*!' hissed Oliver fumbling himself from embrace and stepping away.

Austin came through the door. 'I thought perhaps some Camembert!' He seemed unaware of having possibly intruded. 'Just the ticket, eh? That's what you have with claret, isn't it? And there's some of that Brie left too, I believe. Oh-ho, yes! Connie's taken us in hand with her delicatessen this-and-thats! Getting quite Frenchified we are! Here, I'll carry that.' He caught up the tray. 'After you, Madame. Ladies first!'

Dorothy was still on the sofa, cradling the Moselle bottle. Her glass was again full. Connie set down the plates and forks. Austin delivered the tray. 'I'll fetch the cheese.' He cantered off, passing Oliver who resumed his armchair, inquiring: 'Whose is that?' One red rejected glassful stood on the mantelpiece. Connie said, 'Oh – Mac's or Rowan's.'

'Mine, actually,' said Dorothy pleasantly. 'The children's are over there.' On the sideboard. 'Anyone's welcome to mine,' said Dorothy. 'No foot-and-mouth. Pity to waste it, when it's so real McCoy.' Her face remained innocent of irony. 'Cheers!' she drank some Moselle.

Oliver skewed a swift glance at his mother but withdrew it as he met her bland eye. Austin bustled in bearing cheese. Connie handed plates and napkins.

'You have that,' Oliver told her. 'That' being the stranded glass on the mantelpiece.

'I'm on white, thanks,' she said. She transferred the glass in question to within Oliver's reach. It was still there, untouched, when around midnight eventually the evening closed. It went on the tray back to the kitchen where Dorothy serenely emptied it down the plughole.

The other glasses were consumed, Mac's and Rowan's, and the contents of both vintage bottles polished off by the two men. Austin waxed jolly, and insistently gallant about 'our girl'. Full of applause for her accomplishments. '. . . did all the driving and superbly well, I may say! That's a very comfortable car but not an easy one to park in crowded car-parks! . . . Organized our picnics, no fuss or bother . . . She was telling me about your unfortunate American friend, explained the full force of the McCarthy business – I'd assumed it was a dead issue now the Democrats are in . . .' Oliver matched compliment for compliment. It was a duet. A celebration of a paragon. Oliver said: 'She can handle any vehicle. Motor-bikes included – oh, didn't you? Yes! And that old Morris Cowley double-declutch job – well, you remember that . . .' Cooking? Catering? 'You've never tried her roll-mop herrings, have you? Superb! Better than any delicatessen – well, we'll get her to do some for you.' Political nous? Acuity? 'She rocked the boat,' at a dinner-party in Hampstead, 'hoist the old windbag with his own petard, quoted Kennedy at him: "art is not a form of propaganda, it's a form of truth!" Not bad, eh!'

She sat on the leather pouffe steadily swigging plonk Moselle, her own supply. Across her the two men conducted their duet. Or was the word duel? She might just as well not have been present. She had no existence for them. Sitting on the side-lines as the paragon was batted back and forth, she might as well have gone to bed, to London, or the moon. As indeed might Dorothy. Connie smiled blearily across the tray between them. Dorothy smiled hazily back. From time to time someone or other took titbits from the tray. The talk now seemed to encompass astrophysics, but the paragon appeared to be still in there somewhere, Connie had lost track. Dorothy had emptied her bottle and her glass. She now dozed off. What was Austin making of it all, what had he done with his anger, his contempt – if that was what it had been? Master's lost his fiddling-stick . . .! Did he – get it? Understand the *double entendre*? It *was* a *double entendre*, wasn't it? Though whoever would have *dreamt* Dorothy to have been capable? The closed eyes opened and met Connie's. One eye closed, winked. Then both shut again. It *was* a wink, wasn't it?

More than half drunk by now, Connie foggily recalled Lewis Carroll, Dorothy as the Dormouse. Austin? Well, the March Hare, since Oliver naturally qualified as the Hatter. Which left herself as Alice, who at the end of the Mad Tea-party, confused and tired of rudeness, got up and in great disgust walked off, if Connie remembered correctly. And the last time she saw the others, who had not taken the least notice of her going, they were trying to put the Dormouse in the tea-pot . . .

'What?' Austin or Oliver, one of them was asking, both looking at her.

Connie blinked, gulped the snort of laughter which

was just escaping, and extemporized loudly: 'Tea? Tea anyone? Or coffee? I wondered if anyone'd like –' Runaway mirth threatened again, she gagged it back, standing up. 'Anyone?'

Dorothy, eyes closed, said: 'Tea would be lovely. I'd-love-a-cup-of-tea.'

Connie balanced herself carefully away. In the kitchen she swilled cold water over her face.

In the bedroom Oliver came at her. 'Mmmm, honeybun, honeybun, c'mon, hmmm ...' his hand up her skirt, burrowing. He had her against the wall and with his other hand was detaching his belt. 'Jeeesus! You smell wonderful! Uh ... uh ... c'mon, honeybun!' He'd not called her this for – years, was it? More than months since the last time. Dotty private mumblings, prelude to sex, or sometimes sex, the full treatment; sometimes not. 'Honeybun!'

But then inches away behind her head the clumpherings and rustlings of parental preparations for sleep – a cupboard closing, a spectacle case being set down on a bedside table, a shoe jettisoned; further off, the cistern flushing; and close again an arrival, monosyllables.

'Sodding hell!' Oliver thrust away, released her.

Connie did not then or ever know whether, had domestic geography been otherwise, they would have made love that night, she and Oliver. Or whether foreplay would have also been finale. Or if so, who, which of them, would have been at fault. Or whether it would have made any difference if they'd made love that night, any difference to later events. Or when they did not make love that night, whether she was vastly relieved or bitterly confirmed in disappointment and distrust, discarded? She often thought about it, after; the questions seemed apposite. Answers might have delivered her from the paradox that shadowed her down the years: always, from first meeting, she had required Oliver's commitment, wanted his presence, literal and figurative; needed him near. But equally, she did not. For in some profound way, she was enhanced, not diminished, by the distance he instinctively enforced. Conundrum. And recipe for dissatisfaction. Requiring his presence, relieved by his absence. So. Whether that night she felt once more relieved or once more aggrieved, she did not know. But within moments they had tidied away the familiar shambles and taken refuge in shared suppressed laughter, the comforts of derision, singly tucked in single beds whispering hilarities about '. . . horrendous lives in piggy little bungalows . . .' And – a sop to Cerberus – he murmured across the darkness: 'I'll get at you when we get home!' and chuckled. She chuckled too. 'Have your wicked way . . .!' she complied.

He didn't though. They didn't. Well, it was a hell of a journey – wet, hot, and the traffic God-awful and they were absolutely bushed; Connie certainly was, whacked. Well, they both were. It was true.

And then next day if it wasn't the phone it was the kids or panic over a red-alert bill, the electricity overdue, and the washing, two weeks' worth and a plague of flies in the attic, disgusting, revolting – 'like something out of the Old Testament' as she heard Oliver telling someone during one of his phone calls. One of these resulted in an invitation. 'Next Saturday. All of us. Lunch in the garden, lots of people bringing their kids too. I said yes. You'll like it, smashing house, swimming-pool, and you know Corinna – not a bit Grand!'

In the Rolls-Royce belt, out Sunningdale way. Connie wore her white piqué. Was it suitable? She hoped it was. The week had been busy to busting, kids on holiday, Oliver back at work, busy to busting too, but the amicable ease prevailed between them, even though it had not yet accommodated anybody's wicked ways – but things were harmonious, relaxed, and furthermore Oliver was coming too, to Wickenwood. This time, yes, he could make it. 'Do my stint in the in-law stakes!' He and Connie wryly laughed, had a little hug. 'You'll meet Snowdrop, Daddy.' The grey pony, Rowan's favourite at the local stables they frequented. 'No, *grey*, Daddy! You never say "white" for horses!' He'd not been down in Wickenwood, except for forty-eight hours at Christmas, for almost two years. 'It's just for the weekend, the Fair. I wish you'd come. I wish you would,' Connie had asked. She looked at him, meant it; she really wanted him to be there, completing the unit now, this time. He had met her eye, 'OK!' he said. He patted her arm, dropped a kiss on her cheek. 'Yes, I can make that. Do my stint in the in-law stakes!' Nice if the weather held, no great matter if it didn't, but nice if it did and Mac could take Dad up the Mullen to try the kite out. It was holding today anyway, hot already. Connie folded her manicured hands lightly in her lap as the car accelerated past Windlesham towards their destination.

It went very well. Sartorially, all sorts and conditions were present, outfits from the King's Road, from couture houses, from Liberty's and from Carnaby Street, the men in blazers, summer suits, jeans and sports shirts, even shorts, and Connie was neither overdressed nor too informally, reassured on that score. And soon enjoying herself. The children along with others were in the pool, where they stayed throughout except for sorties to the food and drink administered by some excellent catering firm from canopied tables on the terrace.

'Have you met Richard yet? Richard, this is Oliver's wife, Connie. Richard's our magic-man, raising funds, moving in mysterious ways . . .' said Corinna, gently incorporating Connie in the group.

'Hello, Connie.' He had crinkly grey hair and jolly brown eyes and an American accent. 'Hey, Oliver, you dark old horse!' he called. 'You never told me you had a beautiful wife!'

Oliver called back, 'You never asked!' and blew a kiss to Connie, charmed laughter bubbling in applause. She collected more compliments: 'Never! You can't be old enough!' she was told when it transpired that two of the lusty youngers pounding round the pool were hers. 'Oliver, you have a child-wife!' And later, in her diminutive bikini and her Devonian tan glistening from her swim, a comely young man hung his arm about her shoulder and offered to top up her glass: 'Rosé, wasn't it?' and Oliver spoke up: 'Oi – that's my wife you're handling there!' Amid amused attention, the young man

138

raised his hands in mock surrender: 'Ooops! Well – you shouldn't bring such a lovely wife!' And straight back Oliver said, 'I'll remember to bring one of the unlovely ones next time!' and grinned at Connie who smiled happily back, laughter rippling round her. She was having a nice time. The food was perfect. Simple, plentiful, delicious. Expensive, without a doubt. Corinna ran her life on extremely comfortable lines, but was indeed not grand at all.

Connie said, 'This is all terrific, Corinna!' and then blushed, sounding to herself galumphing and adolescent, but Corinna's pleasure seemed genuine enough: 'I'm so glad you could come today,' she said. 'We've seen far too little of you.'

Connie met a woman in the bedroom set aside for female guests to change in.

'I'm Gillian Flynn.'

'I'm Connie Bruce.'

Gillian told her, 'Me? No, I'm nothing!' when Connie assumed she worked at the BBC. 'Just a wife and mother – mere chattel!' There was no sharp edge in her laugh. Connie grinned, 'Oh! Me too!' They walked back downstairs together, opted for a helping each of apricot sorbet. 'The kids tell me it's "delirious", which is their latest superlative – shall we give it a go?' Gillian suggested. Her three were in the pool too. 'Bliss, isn't it?' she said. 'Few hours off duty *and* superb grub, laid on by someone else! Hmm – this *is* good . . .'

They found they were both grass widows a lot of the time. Mark Flynn was a sound engineer with Outside Broadcasts. He was here today, just back from Northern

Ireland, and off again tomorrow for a week in the West Country somewhere. They collected fresh drinks and carried them to the shade. 'Well – *he*'s happy, so that's all right with me,' Gillian said. 'He loves the work. The kids? Well they're used to it, I suppose. They take it for granted he's away a lot, doesn't seem to worry them at all. Well, it's like the army or fishermen or something – kids accept things, don't you find?'

'Oh yes,' said Connie, quite laid back. 'Absolutely. Same with Oliver, he loves what he does, so . . .' She shrugged, insouciant, in the moment believing that like Gillian she was content with the texture and tenor of her life. 'We're Auntie-widows!' she said. 'You know – grass widows, golf widows, soccer widows? Well – Auntie-widows – BBC, Auntie Beeb!'

'Aah! Got it!' Gillian laughed.

'Cheers!' said Connie, and they clinked glasses, toasted Auntie-widows. After a while they thought they'd better wander down to the pool, put in an appearance as responsible mothers. They perched on the poolside balustrade watching the capers.

'They've been in there virtually three hours – they'll dissolve!'

'Grow fins!'

'Webbed feet!'

'Ah, Connie, there you are!' American voice at her shoulder. 'Just came to take my leave – making tracks. No rest for the wicked! So' – he took her hand in a warm paw, bent to leave an avuncular kiss on her cheek – 'see you in a few days. I'm off there tonight of course –'

'Oh . . . er . . . um . . .' she said, bemused, 'off where?'

'Oh, well, it *will* be Avignon after all, though I'll have to overnight in Lyon – I guess you will too. Depends on which flight – anyhow, it's a stupendous villa and we've got the whole damn thing for the fortnight. Must buzz! See you, Connie. Bye!'

Gillian said, 'Something wrong?'

'No. Er, no.' Connie watched Richard's shoulders angling away through the guests. 'Um . . . back in a mo – must just . . . um . . . 'Scuse me a moment.'

But she couldn't find Oliver.

By the time she did she no longer wanted to.

They didn't row, they never actually rowed. She slumped into sullen depths while he rode high on disdain and exasperation. He hadn't known the dates, he wearily insisted – not when the Wickenwood thing came up, not until Corinna's party. That was not what Barry Sylvester had said, Connie told him. Her mode was sulky, defensive. God only knew why! But beyond availability, locked inside her, wild fury raged. Plenty of aggression, but she could never mobilize it.

'Christ, woman! You're so paranoid! Why the hell should I want to double-talk as you put it? Why? Explain to me if you can the ludicrous processes of your cerebrations!'

And she said: 'Because you know you don't have to go.'

'Don't have to go! What d'you *mean*? D'y'think I *like* spending half my life in transit?'

'Yes. Yes. You do.'

'Jeeesus!' Words failed him, the man beset by idiocy, wilfully misunderstood.

It ran its short and sterile course as had other such encounters. She knew that he did not have to go. She knew he would have revealed the Lamentable Duty at the eleventh hour, too late for reversal. She knew that he had known for at least two months that in the third week of August he would be going to France. She knew that there was an invitation for her too and for the children and that, when he said that Richard Chrysler had been either drunk or totally misinformed back at Corinna's party she knew that he, Oliver, was cheating and that he knew that there was accommodation out there – but in any case he had the time-honoured standby: 'We simply could not afford it!' And it hardly mattered by this stage because she had no desire left to be included, lumber tacked on to the cavalcade.

XII

Connie called Rowan into the hall. 'Want a word with Rachel? Yeh – I'm just phoning to say we'll be down tomorrow – you can have extra rides – you can sort out which times and so on, and then I can ring the stables and book, OK?'

Oliver having gone, Connie was hanged if she was going to droop about in Twickenham single-handed, the kids on this endless summer vac, and all their local chums away. They would go down to Wickenwood. Her mother had said yes, that would be all right – without enthusiasm or displeasure. They could turn up two days early and, yes, she understood it was three not four, Oliver would not be coming. The children were pleased. Given that Daddy had to go away, they were pleased to be going early to Wickenwood. They were sorry that Daddy was not coming. But like Gillian's children and children in general, they – well, accepted it without concern. Did they not pick up any of the currents flowing about number 21? Had they not noticed the drop in emotional temperature since Corinna's party? Evidently not.

She dialled Collingford, the Hennesseys. Well that was the point of going down to Wiltshire, so the kids could get together. 'Hello – hello, Elinor.' Naturally she was perfectly aware that any member of the Hennessey household could pick up the phone. It was of no consequence anyway. She was no longer dabbling in intrigue. She was purely simply setting up arrangements for her children. 'Yes. Devon was very good – wonderful weather of course. Look – I've got Rowan here wanting a word with Rachel. We're coming down a couple of days early – uh-huh, tomorrow. OK, here she is.' She handed the receiver to Rowan. For an instant they were there framed together like a composition Mother and Child in the hall mirror. She turned away, went to make a coffee, or perhaps some tea. The kettle took its time. From the hall came the earnest chunnerings of serious horse-talk. She turned off the kettle, poured a gin and tonic. She carried it about the kitchen, sipping, smoking a cigarette, wandered out into the garden. Mac called from the playroom window: 'Can we take the lilo, Mum? For the swimming-pool?'

'Good idea!' she called back. She thought: no need to come back on Sunday, either. Stay down there a few more days if the weather holds. Even if it doesn't. See some of the friends she hadn't seen for ages. Jane Everett, Caro Bowden, Elsa. Long time no see. It would be nice to pick up threads; old, neglected friends. She drained her gin.

Rowan trotted from the back door to the garage bearing riding boots. 'Is the boot open, Mummy? Oh – boots for the boot!' She was primed and happy from her chat with Rachel.

'Yes, go ahead.'

Rowan said, 'I've packed my project, Mummy!'

'Good.'

Rowan had been going to take it down to show Granny and Grandpa Bruce but she'd forgotten. She had remembered it now, to pack it for Granny and Grandpa Geddes. 'Mustn't forget it this time!' After all, it was Wickenwood's Fair really, the Peapod Fair, and Grandpa was always asking about exams and marks, and this project had a gold star on it, and, as her mother had said, 'You can't get better than that, Rowbuggs! Clever old you!'

Before turning in Connie heard a weather forecast: sunny intervals and occasional showers, cooler than of late. But she packed the piqué dress all the same – spur of the moment before climbing into bed.

They set off straight after breakfast.

'OK you two?'

'OK!' from the back seat. And away they went. With each mile the deadweight of the last few days lifted and lightened. She put her foot down, accelerating away from impotence.

XIII

'That's a very fine tan you have there!' Betty had dropped by at Wickenwood.

'Good, isn't it? On the wane, alas . . .'

'So Devon was OK?'

'Yes. Yes, it was.'

'And Oliver?'

'There was . . . a flap on apparently. He had to go to town for several days.'

'Ah.'

'What about you lot? When do you go to Kent?'

'Next week.' Betty's parents lived in Kent. 'We hung on for the Fair. Roy's been doing Scouty things anyway, so we couldn't have gone earlier. Stella? She's blooming – gone right off school of course, into furtive lipstick and John Lennon. Well, you'll see her on Saturday. Let's go in the garden, shall we? I get claustrophobia in here.'

They walked in the garden, chatting, having a smoke. Connie said, 'How do you feel about that – coming to live here, when Father . . .'

Betty grimaced. 'Well – long live Arnold, say I!' They stood regarding the house. 'It should be knocked down. Hideous!' Betty gestured, embracing the wider prospect: 'The *area*'s nice – much nicer than where we live now – but oh dear, the house . . . Perhaps we could flog it – just supposing anyone would want to buy it. I mean, just how binding are these entail things? What a daft idea it is, entail!'

Connie laughed: 'Not as if it's Chatsworth or something – national heritage material. Grandfather John must have had delusions of grandeur – spot of self-aggrandizement by the look of it.' She was echoing Oliver's opinion, but it was also her own. 'Anyway, you can relax for a few more decades,' she said. 'Father claims never to have had even a common cold. I don't think he intends to meet his Maker yet!' It was a moment of levity that resonated for them both three weeks later at Arnold's graveside.

Betty spoke of mutual acquaintances, local news, as they strolled across the lawn. 'You know about Caro Bowden? No – I suppose you won't have heard. Well, the engagement's off – her bloke's been two-timing apparently – the bastard. Poor old Caro. Yes, one of his students. He was teaching up in Edinburgh – summer school. Anyway, Caro's shattered. Yes, that's right – she'd given in her notice at work, leaving at Christmas, wedding fixed and so on . . .'

'Good grief. That's the second time, isn't it? Wasn't there – ?'

'Yes. Ten years back. But she broke it off that time. She said she didn't feel sure enough, not for marriage.' Betty pursed her lips. 'This time, she was sure.'

'Oh Lord,' said Connie. 'What a rotten business.' She said, 'I was hoping to see her – thought of taking up her standing invitation for coffee, but it sounds as if now is not a good moment.'

'Oh, I dunno – might be just what she could do with. Give her a ring, she'll say if she'd rather not.'

Connie did go to the telephone in the hall that evening and even picked up the receiver, but she put it down again. Perhaps it would be better to drop Caro a note. Telephones can be hard to cope with if you're feeling shaky. Yes, a note.

Caro was in her mind as she drove the children to the riding stables next morning. They had shared a desk at Junior School, she and Caro. They had often got into trouble, talking when they shouldn't. In the winter they both suffered from chilblains – and suffer *was* the word. In those pre-war days school uniform included black woollen stockings, scratchy and smelling of stale soap, and how the chilblains itched – oh the anguish and the scratching. Snow-Fire – that's what you put on chilblains – a waxy ointment in a little cardboard carton with a lurid red and yellow and black design on the lid. Snow-Fire was supposed to stop the itching, but it didn't – nothing did. They would go to the lavatories in break-time and peel off their itchy stockings and plaster Snow-Fire on the swollen blains. The stockings were secured by suspenders to garments called Liberty bodices, curious structures of thick cotton strapped with white tape and sewn with white rubber buttons on which to affix the suspenders ... In the summer they wore white ankle socks; there were girls whose socks remained neat and white the day long, but she and Caroline Bowden were not among them. She and Caroline Bowden were scuffed and grimy by break-time regardless of what they did or did not do. They were among the chronically scruffy whose gym tunics sagged and mysteriously bloomed gravy stains, and whose exercise books crumpled of their own volition, streaked with ink and blotched with nameless sullage. Together they left Junior School and together went on to High school, and through the war years muddled into adolescence – smoked behind the bike sheds, hung about the bus-stop after school to catch the eye of whichever Grammar-bug was currently desired, swooned to Glenn Miller records on Monica Holden's portable, fell in love with anything in uniform except one's brother, and borrowed each other's clothes, illicit make-up and cheap scent. Yes, for ten years and more, they had belonged together, a pair in the wider group, all going separate ways as schooldays ended. This morning, remembering the old days, Connie warmed with goodwill and the intention to see her again. Dear old Caro. Yes. A hug, and a shoulder to cry on if she feels like it . . .

She geared down, rounding the last bend before the stables. The Hennesseys' car was there already; the au pair of course doing the shuttle today, it being Thursday, not the weekend.

But it was not the au pair. It was Alec.

Kit hailed them and ran down the yard. At the car window, he said, 'I can go on the hack!' He was bright with excitement. He looked at Mac, 'Will you come?' He swung an imploring glance on to Connie: 'Oh can he – *please*? Miss Hazeldean says he can if you say so!'

'Oh *Mum*!' cried Mac, 'yes *please*, Mum!'

The hack was the adult ride. It cost a little more and would take longer than the junior ride. Both boys had been getting a bit bored with the junior rides of late and longing to join the adults.

So she must get out of the car and go to speak with Miss Hazeldean.

'Oh yes,' said Miss Hazeldean, 'that will be all right, they can help put up the water and clean tack.' Rowan and Rachel could stay on so that Mr Hennessey and Mrs Bruce need only do the one collection at the end of the hack.

'Hooray! Hooray!' cried Rowan and Rachel.

Alec was looking at her, she knew. She turned at last and lightly greeted him: 'G'morning!'

They stood together and slightly apart, watching the riders mount and eventually move off, the two strings, adult and junior, clattering away down the yard.

'Connie. Connie, my God, that was a long month . . .' He spoke beneath his breath like a ventriloquist, looking not at her but at the stable hands – a man trundling a barrow, a girl unfurling the hose near by. Walking away, he told her: 'Come on.'

At the parked cars he said, 'Meet me at the coppice beyond Sharley. We'll go separately. Take the lower road – I'll park beyond the fork. Oh Connie. Ten minutes. See you there.'

She had not spoken. She watched his car swing away out of sight.

She sat for a moment without turning on the ignition. She assembled thought.

For a month, now, she had been free of the silliness. Silliness was what it was, the trivial flirtation, and the trivial adultery. Trivial, and silly. And life, for all its shortcomings, had been sweeter and simpler for the recognition. And that is what she would say to him. Fond of him, yes. In love, no. And given that both of them were married, well – it hardly needed spelling out, did it?

Yes. That was how to say it. Sooner or later it needed to be said, and sooner was better than later, so she would go to meet him now.

She switched on the ignition. Following the lower road to Sharley, she rehearsed her speech. That was the key word, cutting things down to size: silliness.

'Connie, Connie.' He buried his face against her, holding her so close she almost gasped.

What price the firm intentions? She wondered ever after. It was not his mastery, his expert hands, the rain of kisses, the murmurings – none of that carried her off. It was his humour: he was funny, for the first time humorous. He made her laugh, sending himself up: 'My God, Connie, that heatwave didn't help – hotting up my hormones! I went round in a state of near indecency – d'you know that? What you do to me? I have never in my life been in such a state! Tied to my appendix!' And they were laughing, she was laughing, laughter that was not derisive, laughter that was fun, and laughing she kissed him, in happiness. And 'Darling Connie – darling, darling,' he said, 'now . . . now . . . oh, Connie!'

And it wasn't silly at all. It was wonderful.

'Thanks! Thanks, Mother,' said Connie warmly. Her mother was going to babysit. 'They'll be no trouble anyway – it's just that Caro wants to see me and she's had such a rough time – anyway, thanks.'

'It's all right.' Her mother went on stringing beans. She

didn't look at her daughter. There was nothing unusual in that. Gwyneth rarely looked at anyone she addressed.

'I shouldn't be late back, but no need to wait up of course –'

'No. That's all right.'

Connie was stringing beans too, helping prepare the evening meal. She knew she was talking too much. 'Mac's over the moon about the riding. He's graduated! It's quite a feather in his cap actually – I mean, he's not been riding all that long.' She discarded a bean: 'That's past it – too tough.' She said, 'Doesn't Mrs Birch usually do the veg for you?' and hastily plugged in a jocular laugh: 'Not that I'm complaining – I'm quite happy to be stringing beans and it's a nice chance for a natter.' She seemed unable to stop. Joy and anxiety had come together to release her tongue. Light-headed with consummation, under the greenwood tree this morning, and apprehensive for the evening's designs. Her own. She had told him: 'I'll get out tonight. I'll meet you somewhere. You can, can't you? You can get out?' Yes, he said. Yes he could. And she was going to use Caro as her alibi. She would see Caro, and then go on . . .

Mrs Geddes started on another bean. 'There's more for Mrs Birch to do when there are extra folk in the house. It's a big house for one pair of hands.'

'It certainly is!' cried Connie. 'Well, seventeen rooms! Three extra pairs at least – well, you've only to look at the servants' bells!' she waved a bean at the long defunct row above the kitchen door. 'And the maids' rooms and the housekeeper's in the attics!' She was talking far too much. 'Oh, look,' she said, 'there's a bit of breeze for the kite!' The treetops across the yard riffled their leaves. Mac and Rowan were on the Mullen, trying out the kite before tea.

Mrs Geddes glanced. 'Oh yes,' she said.

Connie shut up. They worked in silence.

Mrs Geddes said, 'Did you get your ointment?'

'Oh!' cried Connie. 'Yes – yes! Got that all right!' She had driven off after lunch in search, she said, of anti-histamine ointment. Midge-bites – Rowan was highly sensitive to midge-bites. And she had bought some anti-histamine ointment. Also, though, that which she had really gone to buy: she could only guess and hope she'd got the size right, for the new dutchcap. Not from anywhere in Collingford. She'd gone right into Salisbury. Taken an hour plus. There had been no comment when she got back.

As for this morning, the risk? Well, chance of one in thousands – no chance, really. Very long odds. But the purchase this afternoon – well, common sense of course.

'Wonderful stuff, Tisanex,' Connie went on. 'Poor child swells up like a balloon and that citronella doesn't really keep the bugs away for long. Actually' – she laughed gaily – 'I think they positively *like* citronella!'

Mrs Geddes sliced a bean. She appeared smaller, more fragile, within the thick woollen cardigan she wore today. 'Leonard Gilray was here this afternoon,' she said. 'Something to do with the car-parking for the Fair, I think. He saw Arnold about something, to do with the Fair.' She said, 'You remember the Gilrays, maybe. They're more Gledwyn's age but you'll maybe remember them. They've parted; she's left him, Alison. She went off with another man, about a month ago.' She spoke without emphasis and without looking up from her beans. 'He's divorcing her now. He's getting a divorce.' She settled the beans in the colander with a weary little shake and stood up. 'It's the children that suffer, though,' she said, and set the colander in the sink, running cold water. 'Anyway,' she said, 'he asked to be remembered to you.'

Connie said, 'Oh, dear – er – oh! That's sad. Yes, I remember them . . .' Across the kitchen she squinnied to read the expression on her mother's face, but found none. Her quickened pulse lurched, then steadied; she measured out her voice in polite concern: 'Yes indeed – it's hard on the youngsters,' she said, and busied herself collecting the parings. 'Oh, here's a bean we overlooked,' she said, and made good the deficiency. 'There we are!'

'Thank you,' said her mother. She said, 'I'm going for a rest now. I shan't want any tea, but you'll take a cup to your father, won't you?'

Connie heard the soft tread on the stairs, the closure of the door above. She lit a cigarette, inhaled deeply, propped herself against the sink. Coincidence, just one of those outside chances – that's all it was. Bit of a jolt all the same. But no other significance . . . Still, a timely reminder, to control her manner . . . Passing through the hall after lunch she had seen herself in the mirror, all assurance and vivacity. She must be careful not to radiate her abounding pleasure.

'*Where* is it you're going, Mummy?' said Rowan, settling for sleep.

'To see my friend Caroline. Not far away – just in Collingford.'

'Is it a party?'

'Oh no – just the two of us. She wants to have a talk because she's been a bit upset. Now, there's your torch if you should need it, OK?'

'Mm. Why is she upset?'

'Ah, because her boyfriend's been unkind – he's let her down.'

'Oh,' said Rowan. 'Isn't she married?'

'No. She was engaged. Now then, sleepy-time! Night-night!'

'G'night, Mummy.' Then: 'Mummy?'

'Yes?'

'You do look nice, Mummy!'

'Oh thank you, Rowbuggs!' Connie brightly smiled. 'So do you! Ni-ni!'

She did not have to use her prepared excuse, because Caroline was groggy with pills and heading for bed: 'It's sweet of you, Connie. Oh Lor' – I'm sorry . . .'

'No no. Really, Caro – *I'm* sorry you're feeling so low. I should have phoned first, but . . . Anyway, look – it doesn't matter a bit, I'll come another time, and I'll ring first . . .'

So Connie did not have to use her fib about not staying long because her mother wasn't well. And within minutes she was back in her car and heading out of Collingford towards the rendezvous; alibi established, she had seen Caroline.

Bold, bright-eyed, on her way rejoicing.

A different rendezvous more distant from home ground

than this morning's. Alec had brought a rug, a thick rug for her to lie on; for them to lie on; though mostly he had lain on her, but also, she on him, the first time she had known it could be so. And the first time nipples had proved so – erotic. She had read in magazines about erogenous zones. Nipples; and other locations. Such surprises, such delights.

No problems back at Wickenwood. Hall light left on for her, everyone gone to bed. Mac and Rowan fast asleep. Connie slept too, deep and dreamless, and woke wide awake in some early pre-dawn hour, mind and body keyed and fizzing towards next time.

XIV

Fair day dawned cloudless and dewy. Good. She would definitely wear the piqué dress. And the emerald espadrilles. Not the Italian silk wrap. That she had not packed. Connie took the dress from the wardrobe and tiptoed downstairs with it. Wearing only her dressing-gown, a mug of tea beside her, she carefully ironed the creases from the piqué. Back in her room, she sat at the dressing-table, plucking and shaping her eyebrows and then painting her toe—nails. Fuchsia. Deep pink. Not that toe-nails were visible under the espadrilles, but they were when those were taken off ... Through her mind, over and over, ran the old tune: 'Small Hotel'.

There's a small hotel,
With a wishing well
Di dum di dum di
Dummmm to-gether. . .!

They were going to a hotel somewhere, soon. Overnight, if possible, and it *would* be possible, anything's
possible if you apply yourself! Yes. A proper bed. He had
made her laugh, he was very sweet and funny, he said
that they needed a real bed. Under the Greenwood tree
was better than nothing but certainly had its limitations,
and talent like theirs demanded the proper equipment.
'It's bedtime!' he had said and that was really witty –
very funny. She softly laughed to herself, waiting for the
nail varnish to dry, admiring the prettiness. Beyond her
bedroom door the household was stirring. She dressed in
jeans and T-shirt and went downstairs to join the humdrum domestic morning, savouring as she went the knowledge that Alec took risks to be with her. Small hotel. And
turning up at the stables yesterday, somehow extricating
himself from the office once he knew she was down at
Wickenwood: 'I wasn't going to wait yet another endless
day, was I?' He'd spun some tale about having to go to
the other branch. He told her that selling one's soul to
the Company did in the end yield advantages – as an
executive he could rearrange agendas . . . Yes, he took
risks, for her.

'Morning, Mother,' she beamed. 'Everything all right?
Thanks ever so much. I'm really glad I went. Uh-huh –
she's pretty cut up, but the doctor's put her on tranquilliz-
ers . . . Yes, just for a week or two, you know . . .'

Betty and Gledwyn drove over from Westbury with the children to take Fair Day lunch at Wickenwood. Christmas Day, Easter Sunday and Fair Day, the three immovable feasts as laid down by Grandfather John. Under Arnold's regime the occasions fell short of festivity. The food was dull, the vegetables were overcooked and libations strictly non-alcoholic. But today Betty had brought two bowls of glorious summer pudding she had made, and a quart of Jersey cream, so that the meal ended on a note almost cheerful – assisted perhaps by the temporary absence of Arnold, who had been called from the table to attend to some question connected with the Fair.

Returning, he announced, 'That was Gilray. Trouble with trespassers. Apparently,' he grimly informed them, 'some unsavoury characters camped overnight in the car-park field. Slept in their car there.' He cast a dyspeptic eye at the pudding and declined a helping. 'I have given him full authority to turn them out.' He unshipped his pocket watch and consulted it. 'One thirty-five. I have told him that if they are not off my property within twenty minutes I shall send for the police.' He restored the watch to his waistcoat pocket. 'I fancy that should see them off.'

'Where have they come from?' said Betty.

'Layabouts,' was the only answer she got.

Lunch being at an end the table was cleared. Mrs Birch set about the washing-up. Gwyneth retired to her room. She was not well enough to put in an appearance at the Fair today. Arnold would officiate, opening proceedings at two-fifteen as had his father before him. John had relished the ceremony, enjoyed the role. Arnold almost certainly did too inasmuch as it nourished his self-importance, but it was disapproval that he made apparent, duty done for duty's sake, an unwelcoming welcome to the multitude. The polite applause from the respectable element would suffice to drown out more spontaneous responses from the rear, 'miserable old bugger' usually being the readiest to lip.

'Come on, you two!' Connie shepherded Mac and Rowan up the stairs to wash and change; and shed her own jeans and T-shirt in favour of the glamorous dress.

She couldn't find him. Five acres and several hundred people here already.

'My dear! How glamorous!' Elinor was smiling into her face. 'Isn't she glam?' she said to Jane Everett who was with her, and Jane said, 'Hello, Connie! I say, you are looking well. Good holiday? Devon, wasn't it?'

'Such a glam outfit!' said Elinor. She said, 'Are you looking for someone?'

'Oh no!' said Connie. 'Just getting my bearings – we've not been here long.' She said, 'The chap on the gate says it looks like being a record turn-out.'

The tannoy system crackled, gave a squeal and adjusted to produce a voice inviting those who had entered garden produce to proceed to the main marquee where the certificates had been awarded and set in place.

'Ooh! That's us!' said Elinor. 'Well – contributors, not necessarily winners!' she laughed. 'I put a couple of roses in and Jane's entered some superb plums – so, 'scuse us!' She made to go. 'Or of course come with us, Connie. But

158

it's not really your thing, is it, gardening? Other things more interesting to you, I expect!'

'I'll go and find the kids – dish out more pocket money.'

'Yes, of course,' said Elinor.

Jane said, 'Let's meet later though, eh? Ages since we had a good chat. How about the tea-tent? What time is it now? Well then – how about quarter to fourish?'

'Lovely,' said Connie. 'OK – see you there, quarter to fourish.'

'Bye for now, then.'

'Bye!'

Connie stood, reining in the impatient need to resume her search, but her eyes were already on the move when Elinor, back at her side, said, 'Alec's taken two of our tiddlers off to the roundabout. When you see him, tell him I've gone to the main marquee, would you?' She was smiling, head cocked, like a bird. Then she was gone.

Did Connie then, at the time, register the whisper within the message – or was it only those weeks later that perception picked up the code? She did notice something then and there, she noticed the birdie bright eye and the sleek cocked head, a perky bird in an Eden of worms. The imagery amused her, at the time.

They stood side by side but not touching, she and Alec, not needing touch, content in the repletion and the greed they shared; they watched, smiling at the children, who dipped and soared on their painted ponies hurdy-gurdied round to the strains of 'Daisy, Daisy, give me your answer, do-o-o-o'.

*

Bolstered by children they moved together through the Fair, an unexceptional pair of adults attending various young. From time to time a glance passed between them, confirming a union infinitely more exciting. And, the while, the children were supplied with pennies, ice-creams, helping hands, lemonades and every assistance in pursuit of Fair Day frolics – Rowan and Rachel, Kit and Malcolm and a small, chattering mob of others, some from the junior ranks of Hennessey, some assorted playmates. Roy and Stella were briefly of the party at the dodgems, but being slightly older went off in search of higher things when Punch and Judy was voted the next desirable treat. Then it was donkey rides. This meant waiting in a queue, so Rowan and Rachel filled the time by haring off to win diamond rings at hoop-la, and Kit and Mac decided that donkey rides were too tame anyway and opted out to go and see the Strongest Man in the World. Two of the smaller girls fidgeted for a visit to the lavatories and Connie escorted them. Donkey rides were satisfactorily in progress when they got back. Alec was buying ice-creams from the nearby van.

'Want one?' he asked her.

'No, ta,' she smiled.

The small girls took theirs to suck in the queue. Alec bought himself a jumbo ice-cream cone. Taking a lick at it and side-stepping a large, shirt-sleeved man who was ordering six chocolate wafers, Alec brushed against her and her pulse surged, the touch rocked through her. 'Connie. Oh Connie.' He kept his eyes from her but the voice was all over her, every inch. 'That dress – those tits!' His murmur swelled with sexy mirth: 'I'm in real trouble – these pants are too tight!' She had never wanted anything so much as at that moment she wanted sex with him. Between pain and laughter she turned to him. The ice-cream cone was raised erect; he held it there; her tongue stretched out, right out, and she licked, lolloped, his ice-cream cone, looking right into his eyes.

'Oh *Mummy*!'

'Rowan!'

'No, darling, of course she doesn't!' Alec reassured her again, telling Connie what she needed to hear. He was totally relaxed, unworried. 'She's nine, darling! Of course she doesn't!'

She wished she was reassured.

A little later she said, 'Look, I think I'll just go and spend a bit of time with her . . .'

'OK,' said Alec, easily. 'Don't *worry*, sweetheart.'

Rowan's face swam before her as she went, Rowan's eyes staring, then darting, to Alec, to Connie, to Alec, back again. And her open mouth, silent.

Alec was right of course – a nine-year-old – and goodness! What of it? Licking an ice-cream!

And she had been perfectly all right, going on her donkey ride. Perfectly happy!

She had simply meant that sharing ice-creams was unhygienic like sharing spoons or mugs.

Skipped off with Rachel quite happily after the ride.

Where is she?

Where?

'Oh, there you are Rowbuggs!' she smiled, keeping it light. 'What's this, Rachel? Oooh – clever you!' A pat on the head of the ugly celluloid crinoline lady won at roll-a-penny. 'What are you up to now? I've not seen the Pets' Corner yet. Come on!'

Several of the exhibits had been taken somewhere cooler, or perhaps taken home. 'Oh!' said Connie. 'Still, there are some left – look!' A couple of angora rabbits hunched in a hutch; a puppy whimpered at the wire mesh; four guinea pigs slept among bruised scraps of lettuce; someone had spread a newspaper over the cage housing a budgerigar. The woman in charge explained that the prize of a five-shilling postal order had been won by a litter of sweet little kittens, but they had just been collected by the owner. 'You've only just missed them. What a shame!'

'Phff – it stinks here,' said Rowan, and walked away.

But she was all right, because she had been laughing and jolly when they stopped to watch the terrier-racing at the main ring. One of the terriers refused to turn forward in his starting-stall and instead of a furry face there was a furry backside and Rachel and Rowan had laughed and laughed. And they had laughed too when in the next race a terrier had overtaken the quarry, run right past it and out of the ring. Everyone roared with laughter. Including Rowan. She was all right. And perfectly cheerful, going off to have another go at Roll-a-Penny so that she could win a crinoline lady too. Not a flicker when Connie said she'd see them later then, just going to find Auntie Betty.

And she had seen Betty and spoken to her briefly: 'How's it going? Just been watching the terriers – absolutely hilarious! They're always good value, aren't they?'

And soon on her way again, seeking Alec.

And there he was, about fifty yards away outside the refreshment tent, with the Renshaws, the Dickensons and Elinor. He had his arm about her as the group stood chatting. He looked down at her. She raised her face to him, and he kissed her, his wife.

Connie retraced her steps, went quickly out of range, not to be seen seeing them. He was keeping up appearances of course.

And anyway, neither she or Alec had ever talked about their marriages, their spouses. Not specified anything. That had not been part of it.

Near the crafts tent she was waylaid by the Reverend and Mrs Downey, who inquired after her mother's health and went on to ask after Oliver and then young Malcolm and little Rowan. At last she got away.

No, that had not been part of it. Well, until yesterday there was nothing . . . Nothing, until yesterday. Could it be only *yesterday*? She caught her breath, amazed by the irrelevance of time. For almost a year they had been – just – playing with flirtation. Sure, he had said, 'I love you.' And they had been to bed in that horrid place in London, but until yesterday . . .!

One day. After a year of nothing!

It was – astonishing! Marvellous.

This time he was alone. 'Oh, *there* you are!' He stepped towards her. 'All right? Rowan all right? There! You see?' He smiled into her eyes. He steered her into the walkway, strolling her along. 'Listen, darling, tonight – I'll be back here at the Fair about eight. OK? I'm taking the kids home soon. Back about eight.'

'Eight,' she said. 'Where?'

'Look, how about if we meet somewhere else – not here?'

'Not here? Oh, but if I take the car . . . I'd have to *say* . . . that I was going out!'

'Of course – oh, damn! OK, then, how about . . . how about that shed . . . at the back – behind the Mullen?'

'The sheiling? Yes! Yes, I can easily get there.'

'Oh Connie.'

'Alec,' she said, 'I love you.'

It was only during the evening meal in Wickenwood's dining-room that she remembered that she had forgotten to go to the tea-tent at quarter to four. But – well, it was not important. Didn't matter.

No part of the afternoon remained in her consciousness as together in the sheiling they abandoned themselves to lust.

At the other side of the hill, the forces of Law were on the move. Cannabis was in the air; Arnold was triumphant; and Peapod Fair was closing down.

Myocardial infarction was the cause of death. Arnold had had a heart attack; but as to why, exactly, remained a matter for speculation – he had seemed in his usual well-regulated health.

Oliver said to Connie, 'Not a damp eye in the house!' They were driving back to London after the funeral.

Connie raked together the sardonic laugh appropriate

to the observation. She was preoccupied. The future was suddenly derailed. Betty and Gledwyn had now inherited Wickenwood. If Betty had her way, the entail would be broken and the place sold up. If not, she and Gledwyn would be moving there. Either way the practice of recent times was at an end; assignations based on Wickenwood were now out of the question – Mother and Father, remote and incurious in their separate stockades, had served her requirements well. Betty, convivial and perspicacious Betty – quite another matter ... Her father's demise had not touched her; inasmuch as she had considered her mother, it was only to notice that she did not seem especially upset, and to suppose that she would now live with Betty and Gledwyn, wherever that might be ... And Wickenwood would not serve any more. What were they to do, she and Alec? That was the question ...

'... huge relief, presumably!' Oliver was developing his estimation of Gwyneth's response to sudden widowhood. 'Impossible to tell of course – after a lifetime of submission she's lost the knack of self-expression.'

Connie obliged: 'That's true,' she said.

And what about this Germany thing? Alec hadn't mentioned anything – they had contrived to meet twice in the three weeks since the Fair but he hadn't said anything about Germany! After she had heard it – overheard it, someone talking this afternoon as she passed among the funeral guests offering plates of sandwiches, someone referring to Alec's 'promotion', and then this 'conference circuit', and 'a month – nice work if you can get it!' After she had heard it, she tried to get a moment alone with him, to find out – she had to know! But it didn't work out and she still didn't know – but it had sounded absolutely certain. But he had not said anything to her . . .

'. . . bit hard on Betty, eh? A gruesome house and a comatose mother-in-law *as well* as the mildewed remains of an improvident wartime marriage – Malign Fate overdoing it a bit!'

Connie kept Oliver supplied with suitable responses.

It was better than nothing but well short of good enough. Half an hour at some pub near Waterloo, the best they could between them manage. 'I'll ring you from Düsseldorf – course I will, darling. Darling girl. I shall need to hear your voice.'

They left their drinks unfinished. Behind the pub amongst the beer crates and the dustbins they kissed and fingered and fumbled, frustrated. He had explained to her, though. She had taxed him, 'Why didn't you tell me?' and he had explained. He had only himself heard that morning, a phone call as they were setting out for the funeral. Well – yes – in a way he supposed it had been on the cards in the long run, but he had not been expecting promotion, not for ages. 'No one was more surprised than me!' She couldn't quite leave it alone; she picked at it: how often, these trips? For how long – always four weeks? Good gracious no. Well, usually four days more like. This one happened to be a double – Germany first, then on to Bahrain. 'And when I get back, we'll have our small hotel!' They named dates, in November. He knew of a place, in Berkshire, back of beyond, he would fix it all up.

She sat in the corner of the carriage smoking a cigarette and watching the bulk of Battersea Power Station swing slowly round and disappear as the train squealed over the points, heading for Twickenham. She had told him again, 'I love you.' 'I love you,' he said. And she said, 'I love you!' Every time she said it, she felt the magic of the words, their power ennobling their relationship.

It was to be on Saturday. All arranged: Mac and Rowan weekending with friends, Oliver away in Paris. They would meet at the railway station four miles from the inn, leave her car there, go to The Choughs in his. Mr and Mrs Young. 'As in the song "You Make Me Feel So –"!' He made her laugh again, telling her all this on the phone. Oh, she had missed him!

On Thursday night Mac ran a temperature. In the morning it had risen further.

She hardly knew which was wilder, her anger or her despair.

On Saturday morning, as arranged, he rang 'to synchronize watches'. He rang from a kiosk somewhere.

'I can't believe it . . . !'

'Neither can I!'

Mac was better by Sunday morning. 'Fat lot of good that is!' she thought bitterly.

They did it in the back of his car. Exercised their lust; made love. Two weeks after the cancellation. On the back seat of Alec's car, on Wimbledon Common, rain battering and streaming in the driving wind, late rush-hour traffic seeding the night with beads of light tracing the boundary road. A poor substitute for The Choughs, but much, much better than nothing. Unexpected opportunity, hastily grasped. Alec was in town for the day – not the night this time, a last-minute call to a business meeting. He would come up by car, give them more leeway – and indeed, a bed of sorts. And she? Babysitters at such short notice? Well. Irony of ironies . . . Oliver, actually. Oliver was grounded, laid out with a king-size head cold and flaming tonsillitis. So.

Actually, it made her feel a bit – grubby. A bit. Not enough to have weighed against the alternative, not enough for her to have said, 'No, I can't' and stayed at home. She concocted a tale about an Oxfam meeting.

One day soon she would tell Oliver. She gave herself easeful moments, conjuring the notion of herself telling Oliver. Not confessional. Simply truthful. Not apologetic. This would be a prelude to a dignified solution agreeable to all, no casualties, no real casualties could result from something so – wonderful.

In the back of the car they did it. Putting clothes back on, elbows and knees awry, awkward. But in another eight days, The Choughs. And this time, surely, no hitches?

Oliver was asleep, capsized in the armchair in his dressing-gown, television flickering and burbling to itself, empty tumbler, almost empty whisky bottle by his side.

She left him there, television and all, and stole up to bed. She hoped he would be better soon, back to work. She liked to be on her own. When he was around the house she could not quite relax, have her thoughts, put records on the gramophone: a Beatles LP. The Peggy Lee album, the track of 'Mr Wonderful'. . .

That image, of Oliver capsized in the armchair, returned to her ever after, time and again, trailing with it a ball and chain of ponderous emotions. Asleep, off guard. Stripped of animation, the mouth lay slack as though surprised by disappointment. As though he had found what he wanted, but it was not desirable after all. He looked older than his forty years, the birthday just passed. Approaching it he had revealed his fear and apprehension, joshing and joking about male menopause, 'watershed time', 'downhill all the way now'.

Once – just the once – a long time before, she had spoken the magic words to Oliver: 'I love you,' she told him. It was his twenty-sixth birthday, and the first since their marriage. She took a cup of tea to him, in bed, and gave him the present she had bought, a volume of Henry James's short stories, which pleased him. And she said to him, 'I love you.' Oliver sent that packing, pronto. 'Nonsense!' he told her. A brisk offhand rebuttal, someone dismissing tales of fairies at the bottom of the garden. He himself had never used the words. Not to her, anyway. She had felt the determined omission, lived resentfully with that. Later, a long while later, she was to review it in a different perspective and to allow him the honour of his own integrity: that was part of his Truth, that he did not love her. And had she loved him? Or had she just wanted to? Perhaps he would have liked to love her. Perhaps that was part of the perplexity, the surprising disappointment with life, which in sleep he was powerless to conceal.

Bedtime; and it was a lovely bed, big. She loved the smell of him; she told him so. 'Pheromones,' said Alec, nuzzling and smiling, kissing her.

'Pheromones?'

'Hmm! Personal chemistry. I love yours too!'

'That's the perfume!' she laughed. 'Je Reviens!' He had given her the flask of Worth perfume, a 'hello again' present when he came back from Bahrain. Je Reviens.

'That's nice too. But I mean you. Your pheromones!'

And they made love.

It was love. Harmony and happiness. She understood now, one of the cognoscenti now, she recognized real love. 'My true love hath my heart and I have his . . . There never was a better bargain driven.'

They slept a little, woke and loved again, and again slept, content, side by side.

They walked naked about the room if they left the bed. She was at ease with her body, a body that was cherishable now.

In the morning he wrapped a towel about his waist in which to receive the tray of coffee they had ordered; Connie kept herself in their pink-and-white en suite bathroom till the tray had been delivered. There was toast as well.

'I didn't expect toast.' She tucked in. 'I'm ravenous!'

'I'm not surprised, darling.'

'Nor am I!' she laughed.

'It's good for you,' he assessed her.

'The toast?'

'The sex.'

A tiny discord threatened. 'Love-making,' she said.

He smiled, lit a cigarette, and lay back watching her finish her toast.

There was nothing to get up for, everything to stay in bed for.

Later, lying curled against him, she tried to reverse her mind's tendency to stray ahead, away from the present – the twitch of anxiety about her car four miles away in the station car-park; a very unexceptional car, not one anyone would easily recognize, just supposing. She made the effort, turned her mind back to the present. She was calm again. Secure. They dozed together.

'Alec?'

'Hmm?'

'Oh – nothing . . .'

Faint far-off sounds of the hotel's day carried from below. Outside, a car started up and drove away.

'Alec?'

'Darling?'

'Alec – what if – well – what would you say, to Elinor . . . if she found out?' She heard and hated the edge of angst in her voice. She shifted slightly, put a smile on her face, looked at his.

Eyes still closed, he said, easily, 'Oh, I'd just say, "Everything went blank – forces beyond my control"!'

And on the instant she knew.

She remembered some of it afterwards, but not all. Had she shouted? She didn't know.

She remembered recoiling from him; and scrabbling for the towel with which to clothe her nakedness.

She remembered saying: 'She knows, she knows – she knows we're here, now.' But whether she was shouting, or whimpering, she could not remember.

She couldn't remember getting into her clothes, though obviously she had. And somehow getting herself down to reception and ordering the taxi, she remembered ordering the taxi and the woman looking at her and looking away.

She left the perfume. She deliberately left the perfume.

Had he said it, or was it just clear as crystal that, courtesy of Mr and Mrs Hennessey, she had been receiving therapy, poor Connie? '. . . fond of you . . .' He had said that. Which of them, fond of her? Or was it both of them?

She remembered his face, and the surprise with which she saw it was sharp, rather unpleasant, but that the voice mellowed on – soothing, presumably. He had not raised his voice.

It had been good for her. The sex.

Did she say it or did it just roar through her brain unsaid: 'Out on licence, are you? You should carry a certificate: fully qualified – satisfaction guaranteed!'

Had she said it? She rather hoped not. It was pretty pathetic. She couldn't remember.

He was sitting up, knees crooked under the blankets, one arm at rest across them. He was smoking a cigarette. She could remember that; her last view of him in the role of the I Love You man.

XV

She had stopped going down to Wickenwood. That immediate Christmas she had flu and so did the children. After that, Wickenwood was under siege from builders, decorators and electricians, and it was blessedly easy to steer clear. Betty had offered: 'Do come if you need to, Con – the kids will want their riding, I 'spect? We can put you up somehow if you don't mind sleeping with your head in a bucket!'

'Oh no, Betty,' Connie laughed into the telephone, 'honestly, don't worry – Mac's gone right off riding now, and we've found a stables over at Hampton for Row-buggs. Yes. 'Course we'll see you before too long. Give my love to Mother, won't you?'

She cringed through the daily round at Twickenham, hating the Hennesseys, loathing herself. And that mad-dened her – what did it matter? Hardly world-shattering, was it? Petty adultery. If you can have petty theft, you can certainly have petty adultery. It's happening some-where every minute of every hour. And so what? Wash your mouth out and get on with real life. She tried to throw off the shackles.

Pillow talk. The Hennesseys. Perversions, sick games. 'And how was it, Alec?' Confessions and absolutions. Part of their foreplay? Climaxing on forgiveness. Was that how it worked for them? It was obviously a smart ploy, in the politics of Positive Thinking. Time and again

Connie confronted that birdie bright eye and sleek cocked head, the perky bird ... Putting the Power into the Power of Positive Thinking. Subject: Adultery. Subsection: Philandering Husbands. Method: Make it a sharing experience – recognize his failing and tell him so, with understanding and forgiveness. Think Positive! He is a man who enjoys women. *You* are a woman – make yourself *the* woman in his life, for you will surely reap rich rewards in the marriage-bed. And you will never lose him, my dear! ... Time and again she tried to solace herself with parodies of the book she had never read, to ridicule the whole experience out of her system. It didn't work. But then the experience had amounted to more than the dross of petty adultery, for Connie.

She had been panning for gold: I love you.

It's a thing women do. She had read about it in a magazine. And: the thirties are a dangerous age for women. She had read that in a magazine too. Also: People, and especially women, are slaves to the human impulse to confess. Another magazine. So much insight and wisdom for a few shillings at the newsagent.

She told him one Sunday evening. They had been walking by the river, the four of them, she and Oliver and the kids in the summer sunshine; they were peaceful together, at their best with each other. The kids were in bed. She and Oliver sat on the back steps above the garden, drinking bottled beer. She told him. She'd had an affair – well, the beginnings of one. Last year. It was stupid, but also wrong, and she was glad that it was at any rate brief. Mistake. She wanted him to know. She thought it had been a reaction to Oliver's going to France that time, but she was not offering that as an excuse. There was no excuse. Endangering other people's security, the children's. No excuses. 'But I want you to know.'

'Why?' said Oliver. His expression as he gazed out across the garden was – what? She tried to read and understand it. Speculative! She had read it, but she did not understand it. He showed no curiosity. Not 'Who?' Not 'Where and when?' No anger, either.

'Well, because it was a dishonesty – between us, between you and me – an untruth.'

'Uh-huh.'

Silence. But oddly, relaxed, in harmony with the deepening quiet evening. 'Do you want "out"?' said Oliver; almost casual, his tone.

Shocked, she said, 'No! No. Of course not. No!' The garden, the porch, the man beside her, blurred together as her mind reeled – what was happening? Had he heard her properly? Had she heard him properly? What ... what ...? What should be happening, in the confessional? She had not thought about it. As the magazine had said, it was an impulse.

Oliver took a swig of his beer. He did not alter his gaze, didn't turn to her: 'What *do* you want?' he inquired, detached.

'I want for us to be – well, happy together! You and me, and the children – but us, together more. Like today – y'know ...?' She sounded faintly ludicrous, like a voice from an agony column.

'Hmmm,' he made an agreeable, agreeing sound. Then he stood up and stretched. 'Want another beer?' as he

175

moved off into the kitchen. And that was that.

Neither shriven nor condemned. In limbo.

Life at 21 went on exactly as before. The children grew. They appeared to be physically and emotionally lusty and fit, busy with school, with friends, with sports, reasonably companionable together at home, take or leave the odd argument about which channel to watch on television.

At Kingsbridge Austin seemed suddenly older. He quickly tired, had 'odd twinges, y'know, nothing to worry about'. But it was cancer. The doctor was 'excellent' and the local hospital 'very good', and treatment there, while unpleasant, was beneficial. In the second year of his illness Oliver and family did not go for the holiday. By common consent it was recognized that that was a bit beyond him now; and Dorothy was showing signs of the strain she was under. Oliver made a flying visit once, Connie went down twice. A turn for the worse put Austin in hospital, and it was clear that this was the last lap. Connie found Dorothy exhausted and mentally depleted: 'She's terribly vague – can't remember things from one half hour to the next,' she told Oliver.

'Losing her marbles,' said Oliver. But the dark patches high on his face belied the flippancy. His absences from home increased. At home the phone tended to bring messages from Dorothy's neighbours, concerned for her, alarmed by odd behaviour; as when she was found pulling up the herbaceous display in the town gardens and put up a fight: 'I'm doing my weeding!' she insisted.

It was obviously time to take measures. And it was Connie who went down and navigated Dorothy's passage into Torquay's geriatric unit. Dorothy never understood that Austin had died. She did not attend the funeral. To the last, she would explain to anyone who could be bothered to listen that her husband was away at the front, in Flanders.

The bungalow was sold up. Connie went to sort out the contents. She delivered boxfuls of clothes and odd-ments to the Oxfam shop. Furniture was shipped off to the salerooms. In the process of clearing the desk she came across photographs, among them the one Mac had taken of her in the light between the trees, wearing the glamorous dress. She fed it to the flames along with old receipts, and watched it curl and turn to ash.

The framed photograph of Oliver, aged eighteen, close-cropped new recruit in army uniform, a child – that, she took home. 'Look!' she stood it on the sideboard at 21. Oliver glanced and gave a grunt of a laugh. 'What date's the auction?' They had been advised that in the overall circumstances putting the bungalow up for auction would be the simplest and easiest way to sell. The estate agent had named a respectable price. 'That'll come in handy!' said Oliver.

Over the next ten years Connie made the trip to Torquay spring, summer and autumn annually. Dorothy sometimes appeared to recognize her daughter-in-law, fleetingly. Maybe she did, maybe she didn't. Connie went because she wanted to. She had a soft spot for Dorothy, ever since the Mad Tea-party. Dorothy Dormouse, who sang 'Master's lost his fiddling-stick and doesn't know what to doooo'... Yes, Connie felt a kinship there, beyond the in-law connection; and she went to see her demented friend for the remaining ten years of her life. Within those years Connie herself became a widow. The two of them would sit together in the nursing home's glass extension overlooking the sea. Connie would tell Dorothy about Mac and Rowan; sometimes she spoke of that summer, the heatwave, the picnics on the beach; sometimes it almost seemed as though Dorothy had understood. It didn't matter to Connie whether or not she had; that was beside the point. The point was the visit. When they ceased, she missed them.

Within twelve months of Austin's death Oliver had disposed the money from the bungalow 'in investments'; and announced to Connie that he was now ready to divorce her. Perhaps he had not felt up to divorcing 'our girl'. Perhaps he had to wait, till Austin was not there to see. That was one of the many things that Connie would never know.

After the Fair

BETWEEN THE LAURELS it was stuffy, airless. Gledwyn and Connie, each in silence and side by side,
slowly walked its length. They met no one, no Antiquarians busy about the water supplies for the refreshment
tent, no stray family members in transit to or from the
Fair, no one. And then they arrived, stepped from the
shadow into the brightness and buzz of Fair day, Peapod
Field brimming with shifting colour. There were scores,
hundreds; and among them somewhere, Rowan; to whom
Connie must speak. Say – something.

'Wonderful turn-out, Mr Geddes!' The villager man-
ning the entrance booth was greeting Gledwyn with the
deference due to the benefactor, the *pater patriae*. 'Very
popular event. Over eighteen hundred already and more
arriving all the time! Oh – afternoon, Mrs Bruce. Yes,
we're all very grateful, Mr Geddes. Lot of folk here can
remember the old days, the Peapod Fairs we used to
have!'

Gledwyn nodded and bestowed an old man's kindly
smile. 'Good cause – glad to have been of service,' he
declared. But inside the ground he grumbled to Connie,
'I'm going to rest – get the weight off my foot. Hurting
like blazes. Find myself a seat out of this infernal heat
and then I'm off. Back home. No. Don't need you. Go
and do your duty tour or whatever you call it.' He
stumped off into the crowd.

Alone, Connie felt a sudden exposure and lowered her head. Antiquarians everywhere, presumably. Hennesseys somewhere, for sure. Furtive and foolish, she sidled to the produce tent, to do her tour of duty, get it over, beat a retreat. Rowan – see Rowan later. Now not the time and place, anyway . . .

At the entrance to the big marquee she paused, glancing nervily. No one she recognized. Or was that Eithne? Away beyond the delphiniums? Cheered, Connie launched off to join Eithne, the sweet and guileless Eithne, in whose company it would not matter who else she had to meet . . . But it was not Eithne with whom she joined up, nor anybody less acceptable either. By the honey stand she met Jean Partridge. Forty-odd years had elapsed, complexions had faded and outlines lost their edge, but they knew each other at once.

'Connie!'

'Jean!'

Not ever close cronies, but fellow passengers on the school bus for years, and friends enough for Connie to have been invited to Jean's wedding back in 1952. Connie had not been able to go – Mac was yet a breast-fed infant and money was short too, new outfits or fares from London beyond the Bruces' means, but she had sent a wedding-present. 'I've still got the bread-board,' said Jean. 'Use it every day!'

'And how *are* you?' they required to know of each other. 'All these years . . .!' Jean had heard, way back at the end of the sixties, of the death of Oliver Bruce. 'I meant to write . . .' She too was now a widow. Ten years ago Matt had died. 'What have you been doing? How are the

kids . . .?' In a while Jean said, 'Let's go and find somewhere to sit.'

'Good idea!'

They decided to try the tea-tent. On the way, Connie
caught a distant glimpse of Philippa; Mac was with her,
and was that Rowan? The shifting crowd obscured them
as Connie too moved on, following Jean.

In a corner of the tea-tent they talked, the two of them,
focusing on the lost years. Jean was the owner-manager
of a small business, Partridge Press Printers, situated in
the converted barn adjoining her old stone house, seven
miles west of Collingford. It had been in Matt's family
for three generations; but Jean was solo now.

Neither of the Partridge sons had joined the business;
one was in the regular army and the other on oil rigs.
Inasmuch as they thought about Partridge Press at all
they thought it was probably time for Mum to 'put her
feet up', retire. 'But I'd atrophy. I love the business
anyway – and it's my home too and I'm not ready to
quit.' On the other hand, to stay competitive she'd need
some new machinery soon and the banks, post-eighties
boomtime, were suddenly very shy of backing elderly
single females; also, the young woman who had been the
second pair of hands in recent years was leaving to have a
baby. 'I've had answers to my ad, but nobody so far I'd
trust with my rarefied hardware! And of course, discretion
is of the essence – my clientele is mostly local to within
ten miles' radius, people know each other but they do not
want their private business bandied about.' It did look
rather depressingly as though one way and another
Mum would have to 'retire'. She was here today because

Partridge had done the booklet for the Antiquarians; and she remembered the Peapod Fair from childhood, so – here she was! And what about Connie all these years?

Well, she'd done this and that, keeping solvent. Eighteen years in Gloucestershire. No, it had never quite come to feel like 'home', though she was content enough, had amiable neighbours, a few friends. She did copy-editing for a small publisher specializing in rural science books. Indexing, too – mostly technical works but the occasional biography or travel tale. She did this at home, and she liked that best, but she had worked elsewhere too. A spell as a dentist's receptionist. A year in a bookshop. That was good – nice couple running it; but they had to close down when the rates were virtually doubled – a lot of small High Street businesses went under then. She'd done part-time behind the counter at a farm shop. A stint at an advertiser paper, but that was forty miles round trip and cost too much in petrol to be worth while. She'd done some indexing here in the last few months, at Wicken-wood. She must get Gledwyn sorted, then back at home she must make an assault on all possible sources of indexing work. Or take a lodger. Or both. Actually, Holmlea wasn't ideal for lodgers – not really the right size and shape, but it could be made to work, she supposed. She had let Holmlea to a couple: 'It's OK for a couple, though less so for two singles.' A husband and wife awaiting the completion of their new house in the next village; they had rented Holmlea for four months, useful in more ways than one – kept the place aired and occupied this summer.

It was the first time Connie had talked about herself and her personal concerns for a very long while. After all, there were not that many people who were remotely interested. Later, it transpired that the same was true for Jean that afternoon. Connie could afterwards recall the sense of easement, a gentle tide of goodwill lifting her off old moorings. Finding herself afloat, but not merely adrift, came later. But over the dregs of tea-cups the talk made its way from the prosaic to the philosophical and Connie found herself explaining that whereas Faith proved pretty elusive and Love a tall order, she could manage Hope from time to time; and Jean was nodding in recognition: 'That's it! Me too. Hope,' she said. 'Hope that life isn't always as meaningless as it seems to be.' 'Correct!' laughed Connie, and added: 'Hope – not optimism, which merely looks for a quick-fix of Bright-Sidery!'

'Oh Lord,' said Jean, 'spare us the Cheer-up brigade!'

'Amen!' grinned Connie. 'Hey!' She was suddenly aware of the time. 'I have to go – Mac and Co are leaving in half an hour. They're only passing through – off on a holiday in the Quantocks. So, I must buzz, I'm sorry to say.'

'Here . . .' Jean fished a card from her handbag. 'Ring me – come over for coffee.'

'I will. Yes. I will.'

Leaving the tent, Connie realized that for an hour she had not given a thought to looming Antiquarians, her mind quit of Hennesseys; nor had she thought of Rowan.

*

Without Gledwyn halting beside her she made a brisk pace up the drive. She had been slightly delayed in her exit, greeted by first the Kents and then the Dickensons, Antiquarians of the amiable and acceptable variety, and she was pleased to have spoken with them. They were nice. But she was late now. Mac and Philippa needed to be away.

The yard was full of people. She stopped in her tracks.

The bonnet of Mac's car stood open. Central to the scene was Mac, bowed above the engine. Beside him, holding aloft some minor organ of the car's anatomy, was Alec Hennessey. 'This is where the trouble is, Mac. That's the culprit!' he said.

'Oh Connie!' smiled Elinor, stepping towards her. 'How lovely to see you! Just lucky we were on hand,' she said. 'Alec has such a good tame mechanic – it'll all be put right in no time! How are you, Connie?'

Connie stood welded to the spot. But on the instant benevolent chance delivered Gledwyn. Emerging from the coach-house, Gerry Kepstow in tow, he was calling loudly to his sister: 'What about this, then, Con? Gerry's going to buy the old bus – going to buy the Armstrong Siddeley. Wants it for his Vintage Collection!' He was in robust form, and forgetting to limp, booming and jovial: 'Vintage, eh, Con? That puts the date on us, eh?'

'Oh, splendid!' cried Connie, equally jovial. 'Yes, it certainly does!' and thus delivered, she went into the kitchen, saying, 'Tea – who's for a cup of tea?'

She made a great number of cups of tea over the next half-hour; glad of the activity, and the to-ing and fro-ing behind which she could muster composure. Gledwyn and Gerry left their tea, vanishing to the study for a more appropriate chaser to the beer they had been drinking at the Fair.

'May we have some Cokes, Gran?' Ruby was here to take fond farewells of Isobel.

'Oh yes – help yourselves!'

Adrian was with Dave, who wondered if there was any cherry and almond flan left because he was hungry.

'You can't possibly be,' said Philippa coming in from the yard at that moment. 'Don't be piggy, Dave.'

'Well Adrian's hungry too,' said Dave. Adrian had nobly left the Laser Clay Shoot with Dave in order to see him off to the Quantocks.

Elinor was in the kitchen now. Opening cupboards for mugs and finding milk in the fridge. Self-appointed assistant in the tea department. Connie kept herself busy. What had she said to Elinor? Out there in the yard. She must have made some response, some appropriate social sound . . . Her first words to a Hennessey in thirty years, and quite unlike those she had once upon a time composed in fantasy to ease her bitter shame, her horrid humiliation. In reality there in the yard she must have said bland acceptable things . . .

Philippa, alongside Connie, said, 'Um – Rowan asked me to tell you – she said to say that she's gone with Alison – Alison someone – she said you'd remember, she used to ride at those stables – anyway, she went off with her to see their new house – Alison's and her husband's – near Over Stacey somewhere, I think. Oh and she'll probably stay on for a meal there and not to wait tonight . . .'

Connie thought: What a lousy thing to do, lumber Philippa, give her the job of passing on lies to me.

Connie said, 'Oh – thanks. OK.'

What else was there to do, or say?

When, shortly, Mac came in and glumly announced that the car could not be repaired until tomorrow morning, Philippa's face fell further than was perhaps justified by a hitch in the holiday time-table. Or so Connie believed. And certainly thereafter Philippa steered clear, was unusually silent – a lady who wished she was out of it and on her way to somewhere else and not stuck with Wickenwood tonight.

By bustling off to find bedding Connie managed to dodge further contact with either Hennessey until the moment of their departure along with Gerry Kepstow. Mac was saying, 'Thanks very much, Alec, thanks. So, we'll expect your chap first thing in the morning, then . . .' And Alec was saying, 'Not at all, not at all! Yes – he should be with you by nine. Glad I could help.'

And Elinor was saying: 'It's been lovely to see you again, Connie! And all your young!'

Alec agreed. He looked at Connie. 'Yes,' he said, and followed his wife.

As she climbed aboard the Daihatsu, Elinor called: 'And we look forward to seeing you in two weeks!'

Connie later discovered the meaning of that incomprehensible remark. Gledwyn, in his philanthropic vein after forty minutes in the beer-tent, had accepted Elinor's supper invitation, for them both. With supreme self-control Connie merely said, 'I see.' She would think of something within the bounds of polite convention, some formula with which to scotch the nonsense – certainly for herself, but also for Gledwyn, who in the cold, sober light of morning would without doubt change his tune. This evening though, he was still in magnanimous mode.

'Jolly nice pair – I'd forgotten, y'know, but Alec was in the RAF too. Good chap, Alec. And she's in pretty fair shape for an oldie, by God! Doesn't look more than fifty. I mean women usually pretty ghastly by our time of life – too fat, too skinny, faces like crumpled paper-bags.'

None of which was likely to improve Connie's present assessment of her brother. She wanted, suddenly and vividly, to be out of Wickenwood. Back in territory that was her own.

At the sink, scrubbing engine grease from his hands, Mac said, 'I'm sorry, Mum – what a balls-up! Look, can I borrow your car? I'll go and get a take-away for my lot, in Collingford.'

'Heavens, lad! No need for that – there's plenty here. And the beds are sorted – no problem at all as far as I'm concerned.'

The young were frankly delighted: Isobel was to share Ruby's attic. They were already up there, undoubtedly still talking nineteen to the dozen. Dave and Adrian had sped back to the Laser Clay Shoot in the Peapod.

Over supper, the Fair was declared to have been a hundred per cent success. Everyone had enjoyed it. The evening settled itself, some opting for a walk, some for television. Rowan's absence passed without comment beyond Eithne's observation that it was always nice to see old friends again. Philippa went early to bed: 'Bit of a headache – think I'll turn in, if that's all right . . .' She raised a smile, at once apologetic and shifty and eyes down, took herself off.

Connie wandered from room to room, out into the garden, aimless, restless. Waiting for the day to finish, waiting to retreat to her own bed.

She was full of animosity, hostile towards her absent daughter.

Connie woke. Had she heard something? She turned on her pillow and peered to read the luminous dial of the bedside clock. Midnight? She levered herself up and switched on the lamp. Two minutes to midnight.

She sat up. *Had* she heard something? She strained to hear, but there was no sound . . . Yet she was certain that there had been sound from below. And it must be Rowan.

She left the bed, shoved her feet into slippers and pulled her dressing-gown about her. Without turning on the stairwell lights she went swiftly and softly down and paused in the hall. She had no speech prepared. She had no clear purpose, beyond the unstoppable impulse to say to her daughter: 'I know what you are doing. I know what you are up to.' To let her know, that she knew her sleazy secret.

Neither spoke. Connie leant against the door she had closed behind her. Rowan stood by the sink, a cup in her hand. In her face Connie read calculation, a readiness to deceive, and confidence.

'Where have you been?' Connie's tone was neutral.

'Oh Lord! Didn't Philippa tell you? Did I wake you – I'm sorry! Didn't Philippa say?' She opened the cupboard, took down the caddy.

'Yes,' said Connie. 'I got your message.'

'Well, then!' Rowan, guileless and at ease, smiled: 'D'you want a tea? I'm making tea,' and moved to the fridge, took out some milk.

Connie's pulse surged. Her heart thudding, she stepped away from the door and stood by the table, erect. 'It wasn't true, the message.'

Connie saw the shift behind the eyes in the fleeting oblique glance.

'It wasn't true, and neither was the party, Sheila's party.'

Rowan set the milk upon the sideboard, closed the fridge door, head now averted.

'Was it?' said Connie. The voice was no longer neutral. The voice was angry.

Rowan turned. 'What is this about?' The smile had gone. But there was no tremor; indeed, she was on the offensive as she said, 'What are you driving at?'

'You're having an affair. You're having an affair. Aren't you?'

Rowan regarded her mother. 'So?'

'*So?*' Connie gasped. 'So? My God, Rowan: so it's wrong. WRONG!' Now she was in full throttle.

'That,' said Rowan slowly and loudly, 'is rich. Coming from you, that is really rich.'

'What? What? What do you mean?'

'Oh come off it Mother, dear. Come right off it!'

'*What?*'

'You,' said Rowan, 'and your squalid affair, with Alec Hennessey!'

It was a real set-to. Connie surprised herself; adept at the oblique variety of combat she had never risen to confrontation, but now she did. A real set-to once it got started. By which time Mac was with them too. Mac had come, tousled from sleep, hunched in his dressing-gown, to sort out Isobel and Ruby. He thought it was Isobel and Ruby, generating midnight noise downstairs in the kitchen. He stood in the open doorway, dumb-struck.

His sister did not rein back; full spate, with barely a glance to acknowledge his presence, she told her mother: '*You*! You talk to me about concern for others! You didn't give a toss for us – you didn't give a damn for Dad –'

At which Mac swiftly closed the door behind him: 'Rowan!' he said.

But she was away: 'Your squalid little machinations – you didn't give a damn – you didn't care when he died!'

'Christ!' said Mac. 'Stop it, stop it, Rowan!'

'Stop it yourself, Mac! Stuff it! You said it yourself and more than once – oh yes! When she tarted herself up, off to her assignations!'

'Shut up! Shut up!'

And Connie: 'Stop – oh *stop*! How dare you! How *dare* you! *Care*! Don't you tell me what I felt when your father died, madam! You know nothing. You know nothing, d'you hear? About me, about your father, about us – don't speak to me about squalor! Standing there dishing out obscenities! My God!'

Mac had sunk to a chair, head in his hands. On it went, the set-to. It had, it seemed, to run its course, this tidal rip of animosity from thirty years ago. 'Stop!' they cried, and 'That's enough!' and 'Shut up, shut up!' But none of them could. Much was said, and perhaps too much, and none of it could ever be withdrawn, not truly erased. Matters specifically relevant, and matters peripheral but lending themselves as weapons in the set-to.

Connie required to know if this 'man' in Rowan's life was married, did he have children? And 'Yes,' said Rowan. 'Like Alec Hennessey.' She added that the difference was that she, Rowan, and her 'man' were in love. In love. Not just having a bit on the side. Connie told her: 'That is what you think now. I know you think you are in love, and that that makes everything all right.' Rowan told her mother that it was none of her business, anyway. 'It's my business and nobody else's!' And Connie told her, 'It is not only your business. Apart from your children and your husband, you have already involved me to serve your purpose – oh yes! And Philippa. Yes, Philippa too.'

And was it then that Rowan returned to derision: 'Who are you to talk? Sitting in judgement!' And Connie acidly observed that given that a verdict had already been passed on her, 'tarting around in a squalid affair', then perhaps that made her specially well qualified to 'sit in judgement'. Or had that come later?

At some point Rowan was telling her mother that: 'Clive is no saint – don't go imagining he's the lily-white boy!' And then: 'You – you don't know anything about us!' An echo, conscious or otherwise, of Connie's earlier rebuke. To which Connie replied, 'Not for want of trying! You tell me nothing. I ask, but you tell me nothing.' And Rowan whipped back: 'You don't want to know about *me* – not really! You want to be told that everything's fine, Mr and Mrs Nice with their nice happy children like something in a Corn Flakes advert!' And Connie, tremulous and indignant, came up with an old grievance: there'd been no interest, no sympathy, no helping hand when she had been on the ropes, losing her home, having to sell up number 21. But then, she had not been invited to Rowan's wedding either. It seemed she had been foolish to expect it: 'I see that now,' said Connie, bitter and self-pitying.

But Mac was saying to Rowan: 'Ruby knows you're having an affair, y'know – oh yes she does, believe me!' And Rowan scoffed, 'Of course she doesn't. There's no way that she could. Don't dramatize!' At which Connie said, 'He's right. Mac's right. She does. Well – children do, don't they? Isn't that obvious tonight? What more proof do you need?' And Rowan veered away from the issue, turning to Mac with: 'And it's not "an affair". It's not a grubby little affair!' And Mac said drily: 'Oh no, I forgot. It's *lerv*.' He told his sister that he did not want to be dragged into it, not even by proxy through Philippa, and that she could leave them out of it from now on. 'Don't worry!' said Rowan. 'I won't ask you to soil your dainty hands, but as a matter of fact Philippa understands. She understands very well. And I'm sure she doesn't need you to make choices for her!'

Mac said, more to himself than to anyone else, that he could remember, he had been aware, that his father was sometimes difficult to relate to, inaccessible – even, sometimes, unkind. And Rowan roundly responded: 'Well *I* can remember Dad being damn good fun!' And Mac said wearily, 'That too. They aren't mutually exclusive qualities.'

On it went. Until the wave evidently spent itself, or at any rate, exhaustion fell upon them. There had been a beginning, but no discernible middle, and no end. Without conclusion, worn out, they went their separate ways to bed.

In the morning Connie thought: as an attempt at Motherhood that left something to be desired. Climbing slowly into her clothes, she thought: moral guidance? Wisdom of maturity? She met her jaundiced glance in the mirror. If memory served, the best she had managed was an aggrieved sarcastic claim to the right to sit in judgement since, as an old hand in squalid affairs, she was well qualified. She had spent herself in defence, offered nothing in support. What a shambles. And yet. And yet. Oddly enough, when they parted, they were in some way closer. Some fences were down; they were all three more vulnerable, but also less estranged. They belonged together.

The tame mechanic came, complete with new part. Mac and he delved and tinkered. Eithne and Philippa stripped beds, and rounded up odd socks and toothbrushes left in bathrooms. Philippa wore an expression of busy concentration, effective in keeping potentially difficult conversations at bay. Rowan, who rose late, wore a similar expression with added designer trims of calm self-assurance. Connie wondered if it was only she who could see the insecurity and fragile defiance just beneath that surface. Rowan left early. She had to 'get back'. Connie knew that she was going to keep her tryst with her True Love. Neither woman looked at the other as farewells were made. It was quite easy to side-step each other in the general mêlée, and most attention was on the joyous news that Ruby was going to the Quantocks, Isobel's ally against the intolerable ennui of the dreaded Family Holiday. Gledwyn nursed his head and his poorly foot in bed. He had set about the claret last night and was the worse for wear. Connie took him some coffee and some paracetamol.

'Here y'are, chuck.'

'Ohhh. What time is it?'

'Eleven. Rowan's gone, Mac and Co are just off. The others are going after lunch. Stay put, if I were you. No need to get up.'

'Oh thanks, Con.'

'I'll bring you some soup later. Have a sleep. Oh' – she remembered to tell him – 'Ruby's been rescued! She's off to the Quantocks. She and Isobel are big buddies!'

'Ah good!' said Gledwyn, and he meant it, his voice rounder and softer. 'Good girl!'

Connie stood at the landing window a moment, looking out at the Mullen. Sounds drifted from the Peapod, the rattle and rumble of lorries and tractors, come to carry the Fair away. And the house would soon be empty, back to its complement of two ageing siblings. As she walked slowly down the stairs, she thought again about the thrashings, which had not fortified Gledwyn's character. Poor old lad, lonely and fearful; all self-esteem thrashed out of him before he had a chance. Poor lad. Also, however, tiresome old humbug. Surely, somewhere in the world, there was a woman of saintly sweetness and thoroughgoing competence who could fill the post of house-and-Gledwyn keeper . . .? She must have another go at the agencies . . .

After Mac and Co had gone, and the happily smiling Ruby, Roy took his progeny down to lend some hands in the Peapod. 'We can pick up litter, if nothing else!' he said and they all seemed perfectly cheerful, trotting off with bin-liners. Eithne and Connie began to prepare the lunch.

'Actually,' said Connie, 'I've just got a phone call to make. Back in a jiffy.' She found her handbag and carried Jean's card to the telephone.

Rowan was often in her mind over the next few days. How was it going? With Clive? With her True Love? And indeed, who was Connie to say that this could not be love? Perhaps it was. And then what? Who is to say which course could wreak the greater havoc: gritting your teeth through a rotten marriage, or going for gold? Which was worse for the children? Or better? True love, the real thing; but Ruby and Teddy outsiders, non-participants. Would it suffice for them to know that Mum had found love that had no place in it for Dad?

She wondered who the man was, what he was like. Maybe he was a good man. He need not necessarily be some predatory Casanova. Men, too, could be romantic. Men too could yearn for and seek the Ideal Relationship that would make them whole. There had been more than a touch of that in Alec. Yes, it was true. It had taken her a long time to concede. But he had not been simply philandering; there had been a faltering quest there for him, too. And remembering the elegiac quatrain on folly, she had an amendment to make:

> When lovely woman stoops to folly
> And finds too late that men betray . . .

She would have to say that her 'melancholy' and her 'guilt' were rooted not in another's betrayal, but in her own. She was, it turned out, responsible for the actions that were her own.

The night before she went over to have coffee with Jean, Connie had a dream. Oliver and she were in the dining-room at Wickenwood. It was the old, pre-Betty dining-room. Oliver was dressed in a corduroy suit. They were both young. There was a suitcase, packed, somewhere in the room. Departure was in the air, and a rising tension. Oliver was saying: 'Five hundred. Five hundred pounds,' informing her of what he was about to take. And in the room the light altered, broadened a little, and she said: 'No.' She said it with sudden resolution and no anxiety. 'No,' she said. 'You can have three, not five.' She was to have the rest. And in the dream she knew she would prevail.

She lay awake in the dark after the dream, looking at it, its extraordinary clarity, the almost palpable presence of Oliver, the shape of his finger-nails, the set of the chin, the quality of glance, at once penetrating and detached. The energy. She heard her voice again: 'No.'

And she did not have less than he. Three from five leaves two. Not even half. But she did not have less, because it was enough. In the mathematics of the spirit, she had enough. And a great tenderness for Oliver filled her: because no matter what he had, Oliver would never have sufficient. And she saw his dilemma, and he was absolved. They both were.

A selection of quality fiction from Headline

THE POSSESSION OF DELIA SUTHERLAND	Barbara Neil	£5.99 ☐
MANROOT	A N Steinberg	£5.99 ☐
DEADLY REFLECTION	Maureen O'Brien	£5.99 ☐
SHELTER	Monte Merrick	£4.99 ☐
VOODOO DREAMS	Jewell Parker Rhodes	£5.99 ☐
BY FIRELIGHT	Edith Pargeter	£5.99 ☐
SEASON OF INNOCENTS	Carolyn Haines	£5.99 ☐
OTHER WOMEN	Margaret Bacon	£5.99 ☐
THE JOURNEY IN	Joss Kingsnorth	£5.99 ☐
SWEET WATER	Christina Baker Kline	£5.99 ☐

All Headline books are available at your local bookshop or newsagent, or can be ordered direct from the publisher. Just tick the titles you want and fill in the form below. Prices and availability subject to change without notice.

Headline Book Publishing, Cash Sales Department, Bookpoint, 39 Milton Park, Abingdon, OXON, OX14 4TD, UK. If you have a credit card you may order by telephone – 01235 400400.

Please enclose a cheque or postal order made payable to Bookpoint Ltd to the value of the cover price and allow the following for postage and packing:

UK & BFPO: £1.00 for the first book, 50p for the second book and 30p for each additional book ordered up to a maximum charge of £3.00.
OVERSEAS & EIRE: £2.00 for the first book, £1.00 for the second book and 50p for each additional book.

Name ....

Address ....

....

....

If you would prefer to pay by credit card, please complete:
Please debit my Visa/Access/Diner's Card/American Express (delete as applicable) card no:

Signature .... Expiry Date...............